ABOUT THE AUTHOR

Andrew Davie received an MFA in creative writing from Adelphi University. He taught English in Macau on a Fullbright Grant. In June of 2018, he survived a ruptured brain aneurysm and subarachnoid hemorrhage. His work can be found in links on his website : asdavie.wordpress.com.

No One Runs Faster than a Bullet

by
Andrew Davie

Close To The Bone
An imprint of Gritfiction Ltd

Close To The Bone
an imprint of Gritfiction Ltd
Rugby
Warwickshire
United Kingdom
CV21
www.close2thebone.co.uk

Proofread by Carly Rheilan
Interior Design by Craig Douglas
Cover by Craig Douglas

First Printing, 2020

Acknowledgments

Thank you to Ellen, Carole, and Susan for reading various drafts and providing feedback.

For my brother, Adam

No One Runs Faster Than a Bullet

January 17th, 1920

ITH THE RATIFICATION OF THE 18th *amendment, Prohibition began in the United Sates. The sale and transport of alcohol were then illegal. Supported by The Temperance Movement, and a desire to address various problems in the United States, the goals of the 'Noble Experiment' were to reduce crime, improve health, and lower taxes. However, as a direct result of Prohibition taking effect, gangsters and outlaws were able to establish a more organized enterprise with which to control their activities. The many new occupations which came into being included the business of rum running or bootlegging.*

January 21ˢᵗ, 1920 : The Rise of Organized Crime

ARNOLD ROTHSTEIN, ALREADY NATIONALLY *recognized for fixing the 1919 World Series between the seemingly invincible Chicago White Sox and the underdog Cincinnati Reds, went on to revolutionize how the criminal element could operate in the United States; he brought it from the era of the street corner hoodlum to the era of the sophisticated gangster. Prohibition allowed for this business to flourish as the desire for alcohol was only intensified by its absence. In order to satisfy people's need, some of the more enterprising citizens distilled alcohol and created what became known as 'Bathtub Gin'. Others drank Sterno, which was referred to as 'Canned Heat'.*

Seeing an opportunity, the underworld took over the business of illegally providing alcohol. Soon, various ethnic groups had been transformed from street corner thugs into organized factions with a complicated network of unlawful activities including extortion, weapons and narcotics trafficking, prostitution, fraud, money laundering, loansharking, murder, and eventually, bootlegging.

The Outfit, under the leadership of Al Capone, ran the rackets in Chicago. The Purple Gang controlled the action in Detroit. Dutch Shultz, 'Legs' Diamond, Frankie Yale, Salvator Maranzano, and Joe Masseria controlled the various gangs which ran the bootlegging operations in New York City.

While Chicago and Detroit handled most of the crime in the Midwest, it was the Kansas City organization which was responsible for the Kansas and Missouri territories. A few years into Prohibition, however, rival gangs began to pop up, and they challenged the Kansas City faction at every turn.

The Weintraub Syndicate had muscled in on the bookmaking, loansharking, and gambling in Kansas. Initially, Schlomo Weintraub had been back east in New York. He'd made his bones as a teenager, and though he was shrewd and had apprenticed under some heavy hitters, he knew he would never ascend to the throne by working for other people. He sought to create a new regime. He moved his family, and some associates, to Kansas City, Kansas where they quickly injected themselves into the aforementioned criminal activities. When Prohibition started, they were all too ready to get a piece of the action.

Weintraub assembled a team of locals whom he and his people would oversee. They distilled and transported alcohol, ran speakeasies, and kept the general public inebriated. The Weintraub's rarely got their hands dirty. Their subordinates handled the majority of the burden, but everyone saw a cut. Politicians and law enforcement were greased. The rest stayed in line through intimidation tactics, and overall business was good. Sometimes, Weintraub's crew would have skirmishes with the Kansas City Organization. They lost a few of these encounters, and they won a few, but there was enough money to be made for everyone, so eventually, they called a truce and established an alliance which lasted for almost the entirety of Prohibition. During this time, the Weintraub family amassed a small fortune, and the syndicate they commanded took a piece of almost every single illicit activity.

October 24th – October 29th, 1929

*T*HE US STOCK MARKET CRASH. THIS EVENT *closed out what became known as 'The Roaring Twenties' in the United States, in which everyone embraced excess in every capacity. Overconfidence in the strength of the market combined with many investors being overextended on credit were amongst the root causes of the crash, which in turn became a catalyst for The Great Depression. Most investors lost all of their money and were forced into unemployment. The panic which resulted from rampant selling only made everything worse.*

October 20th, 1929 : The Black

LBERT CARR LOOKED AT THE TICKER AGAIN. He held the strip of paper between his thumb and forefinger. It probably weighed less than an ounce, but due to impact of the information he had just processed it felt like it weighed much more.

The number couldn't be right. He did the math quickly in his head.

It would mean in a two-day period the Dow Jones Industrial Average had fallen a quarter of the total value. The *Sun* had written extensively about the troubles over the weekend. They had called Monday 'Black Monday', and unsurprisingly they had labeled yesterday 'Black Tuesday'. He wondered whether the trend would follow for the whole week – if the market managed to survive that long.

Albert had felt the urge to get out of his positions when he had the chance before this week, but some feeling deep within him had fought against doing so. He'd seen his share of ups and downs in the market, and he'd been burned before. They'd all been warned. Every year, there seemed to be one sort of crash or another, and the market always rebounded. So this time, he was going to hold on tight and ride it out.

Of course, if the numbers were correct, this was the one time he should have pulled everything out and ran for cover. He looked over the ticker information again; he was through. What would he tell Beth?

It's been great so far, hasn't it? Well, you're going to have to sell everything and live on the streets.

Could he handle putting her and the kids through that? Maybe, if they were lucky, they could go on unemployment. Regardless, he doubted he could ever face them again.

The rest of the office was silent. All of the other brokers had left as part of a mass exodus earlier in the day. Somehow, Albert could not bring himself to do that. He kept hoping a message of good fortune would come over the tape, but so far none had. He knew he was deluding himself; avoiding having to go home to reveal what had happened. He checked the time. Beth and the kids were probably waiting for him in the living room as they always did.

The tears streamed down his face for the last few minutes, but he only realized it now. Albert knew what he had to do. He dropped the ticker tape on the floor of his office and marched over to his desk. The newspaper was open atop his ledger with the ominous headline prominently displayed. He opened the second drawer and removed a Colt Peacemaker. Albert didn't need the weapon for protection, but it was rumored to have belonged to Jesse James, so it was more of a point of pride and a show of wealth. He sat down at his desk and tucked the barrel of the weapon under his chin.

June 23rd, 1933 : The Fighter

EZRA COHEN SAT AT HIS DESK AND STARED AT the forms in front of him.

Some were blank. Some of the stacks had been on his desk for hours; other piles had just started to accumulate. The office air was stale, and he still hadn't gotten used to it. He doubted whether he ever would. He wouldn't admit it to anyone, especially his wife, but he longed for the smell of liniment rub to fill his nostrils again. He shuffled the papers around on his desk. They looked like they would be a headache. Ezra massaged his temples in anticipation. He hoped this would alleviate his stress and delay the headache, which he knew from experience to be looming. His knuckles were still bruised and scabbed. He examined them, and it made him smile. He missed the fights, but he needed the job. So, he had quit the fight game when he had been recruited into federal law enforcement. Guaranteed money was also nice. Of course, it was also better not getting your faced pummeled regularly.

Ezra had been a brawler; a real crowd pleaser. He recalled the details of his last fight against Herman Hicks. They'd fought seven times previously. They had split the first six.

In the fourteenth round, of their seventh and last fight, Ezra had connected with a shot that put Hicks to the ground. Hicks didn't beat the count. He didn't even try to get up. He lay on the canvas and shook violently. He gasped for breath, but the oxygen wouldn't come. He looked like a fish who'd been removed from the water; the only thing missing were the gills. It turned out Herman had broken his nose and cheek. Ezra hadn't even loaded his gloves.

While he got the better of Hicks that particular time, it wasn't as if Ezra made it through the fight unscathed. He was bedridden the first few days afterward, but the beating he had given Hicks made it easier to weather the discomfort; not to mention, it put him ahead in their rivalry. Before that particular fight, he had stayed primarily on the Midwest circuit. He would barnstorm when he could. The majority of the time, he had travelled from small town to small town and fought on undercards of main events whenever he had the opportunity.

He could remember the details of his last fight on the road as if it was yesterday. He stared at the papers on his desk again until his eyes crossed, and the memory of his final fight took over. 'The Arena' in which he was to participate that evening had really been some school gymnasium with wooden chairs set in four quadrants on the floor. The ring may have been built by a shop class of students only hours before the event was to take place. It looked like tons of other venues Ezra had visited during his tenure on the road.

"Just remember; make 'em look good out there but not too good," his trainer, Ham, had said when they settled into the locker room. Ham gripped a toothpick in his teeth, so he spoke out of the corner of his mouth as he wrapped Ezra's hands. Ham tore off a piece of tape with his teeth and fitted it across Ezra's right knuckles to finish his work. Ezra smacked his right fist into his left, and the sound echoed throughout the room.

They'd been working together for about three years as trainer and pupil. Ham had been a one-time promising fighter who had torn his Achilles tendon and couldn't have proper weight distribution anymore. He had become a trainer out of his love for the sport but still needed to earn a living. Enter Ezra. Though a professional, technically, Ezra would never rise to the top of the fight game. It didn't mean he wasn't very good; just not in an echelon which would see his name written in history books.

When he wasn't barnstorming, Ezra worked as a sparring partner. He enjoyed the work, but his true passion lay in hitting the road with Ham. They almost never turned down an opportunity. Ezra would take fights on any undercard; no matter how small the venue. Sometimes – frequently in fact – they'd get paid less than their expenses. However, there was always money to be made from the action inside the arena. Local bookmakers salivated when they saw Ezra's record. They were more than willing to accept bets on everything including how long Ezra would last in the ring before he was knocked out. However, unbeknownst to them, Ezra's record was deceiving. He had a granite chin and could take an unprecedented amount of damage. The art of Ham and Ezra's enterprise lay in Ham's ability to vet the locals who wouldn't give them trouble after the fight ended, if the locals had smelled a fix. Ezra and Ham made it a point to steer clear of connected guys; even those who might have had loose affiliations with the criminal element. Ezra's job was to carry his opponent, and absorb the first few rounds of an onslaught, so Ham could get better odds. They'd been at it for about a year and a half, and so far things had pretty much gone their way. Neither of them had had lofty aspirations when they started, and both knew the business model had no longevity especially with the country in disarray. Too many things could go wrong. But for now, they continued to rake in just enough.

"Alright," Ham said when he had finished applying Ezra's wraps and put on the mitts.

"One, two, three," Ham said and held the mitts in the air.

One meant a left jab, two was a right cross, and three was a left hook. Ezra threw the combination which had been seared into his memory from repetition. His movements were fluid and crisp. Each time his gloved hand hit the mitt, it sounded like two pieces of wood clapping together.

"Again," Ham said.

Ezra threw the same combination, but this time Ham tried to hit him twice with the left mitt in an attempt to imitate a double jab. Ezra blocked both punches with his right glove and circled away. Ezra was neither fast, nor slick, and employed what was known as an earmuff, or peekaboo, defense. He kept his forearms in front of his face. It provided maximum coverage of his more vulnerable areas but at a heavy cost. As a result, it was more difficult for him to unload his own combinations. However, this didn't matter much, considering the game plan. They continued to warm up for another few minutes or so, until Ezra was loose. He continued to shadowbox.

Ezra's fight was the fourth one of the evening out of twelve. When they walked to the ring, Ham helped split the ropes, and Ezra entered. There was a lot of give to the mat, and the ropes sagged as both of them had expected they would. Ezra's adversary tonight was doughy with almost no definition, but that could be misleading. Often on the traveling circuit, like this one, the cardinal rule was to never underestimate your opponent. Some of these fighters seemed soft, but they were incredibly strong. Years of working manual labor had hardened them to a point where one mistake against them could prove your undoing. Certain fighters fed off the pain and enjoyed the masochism. It bordered on insanity. Ezra never took anyone lightly. That's not to say he didn't lose. He frequently did. But, he and Ham always made money even in a losing effort. The announcer said Ezra's name, which drew a few whistles and some profanity. A popcorn bag sailed into the ring, and Ezra kicked it away. The announcer waited for the commotion to die down and said the hometown fighter's name. When the home fighter entered, he addressed the four sides of the ring individually and pointed to the crowd. He was greeted with applause. The fighters and their trainers met at the center of the ring. The referee gave his instructions, and both groups returned to their respective corners.

"I got you starting at four to one," Ham began "Let's bring that up to eight to one, so make nice with this guy for a few."

Ham put the mouthpiece in Ezra's mouth and stepped through the ring ropes onto the aisle. After Ham had left, Ezra felt the familiar sensation of a vacuum form around the ring, which blocked out the sound and slowed time to a crawl. The bell rang, but it seemed distant and far away. Ezra watched his opponent came closer, and Ezra went to meet him. Time sped up until everything was in full swing again. Immediately, Ezra was peppered with three jabs – boom boom boom – which snapped his head back each time. His opponent back peddled away and circled to the left. Blood flowed from Ezra's nose; it had a thick copper taste. Ezra donned his earmuff defense and plodded toward the guy. The same scene repeated itself for the entirety of the round: Ezra would cut off the ring and get tagged with a few decent jabs; both fighters would reset and begin the same process over. The bell rang again, and Ezra returned to his corner. Ham was through the ropes already with a stool in one hand and a bucket in the other.

He pressed an Enswell, a small rectangular piece of metal kept on ice, against Ezra's left eye to ease the swelling and rubbed petroleum jelly above the same eye to help close the cuts.

"What do we know?" Ham asked.

It was what he always asked Ezra before round two began. He could gauge Ezra's faculties, depending on his responses, but he would also know whether Ezra had picked up on any of his opponent's weaknesses he could exploit later in the fight.

"Good jab; loves to circle away from the right. Quicker than he seems," Ezra said and spat crimson into the bucket.

Ham gave him some water, and Ezra spat again.

"Anything else?" Ham said.

"How many rounds, you say?" Ezra asked.

"I'd guess the odds about six to one now, so at least for a few more."

Ezra accepted the mouthpiece and continued.

Rounds two through six were mirror images of each other. Ezra was a sucker for his opponent's jab and ate a lot of them. His head would snap back, and like a snail, he would leave a trail of blood and sweat behind him. However, and it would have been almost imperceptible to most in the crowd, after he absorbed each jab, Ezra would land a subtle right hook to his opponent's body. It wasn't doing much damage outright, but slowly his opponent began to favor guarding that side of his body, which meant his posture had tilted. Ezra's opponent proceeded to spend so much time thinking of protecting his left side, that his right arm had elevated leaving his liver unprotected.

Round seven began, and the odds had risen to nine to one against Ezra. Ham gave him the go ahead to end things in this round if he could. When the bell rang to start the round, Ezra charged to the center of the ring with renewed determination. He took a few jabs for his effort, but he barely felt them. Instead, he had honed in on his opponent from an eye which resembled a ripe plum, and threw his own jab in sync with his adversary.

Both of their heads whipped back simultaneously, and in the confusion Ezra landed a sledgehammer shot to his opponent's liver. The man continued upright for another few seconds as if nothing had happened. Then, suddenly, he grimaced and took a knee; it had been a delayed reaction from the blow. A shot to the liver shuts down the entire central nervous system. The fact his opponent stayed on a knee and hadn't sunk to the canvas was just a testament to his strength and fortitude. The crowd went silent. The hometown fighter had dominated the fight for the first six rounds, and it appeared he would have no trouble coasting to the end. Suddenly, and without any warning, the tide had turned. The referee stopped the count at eight. There was no point in continuing. Ezra's opponent had now fallen to the canvas and clawed at his liver while his trainer did what he could to help. Ezra returned to his corner where Ham took off his gloves.

This final part of their scheme was the most difficult to pull off. Emotions were high and usually fueled by alcohol covertly or sometimes not so covertly snuck into the arena. People who lost money were often not calmed with reason and logic. Ham kept a loaded .38 on his person for dire occasions. Ezra and Ham exited the ring and quickly made their way back to the locker room. In a minute, Ezra had changed in his clothes. They'd made arrangements with an intermediary to hold the money, and Ham broke the guy off a few bills as soon as they concluded their business.

Outside, in the parking lot, was where they would probably find trouble if there was going to be any. Of course, it also depended on how quickly the counter party might feel the need for revenge, or if they even realized they had been fleeced. Ham and Ezra opened the front door and walked out into the humidity. Waiting for them in the parking lot were four men with sour looks on their faces.

"You boys done made a mistake," the first guy said. He had a beard and wore overalls.

The second man in the group was easily six-six. He was a corn fed monster. He would definitely be difficult to handle. The final two members of their party were young; possibly sons or nephews of the previous two and green to these matters. However, they needed to get experience somehow. This would be a good moment to break them into the business. The four of them swayed a little from their intake of booze but looked excited enough to make a decent push.

"Fellas, what can I say? You backed the wrong horse. Just call it a day, and sleep it off," Ham said. He had the .38 tucked in his waistband. He didn't think he'd need to use it this time, but every so often it was helpful to brandish and wave it around to ensure their getaway.

"I don't think so," Cornfed said and rolled up his sleeves.

Ezra's wraps were still on his hands and wrists. He'd already heard enough at this point and walked toward them. Ham remained poised. He let Ezra ply his trade without getting involved. Four opponents were a lot for certain, but Ezra had entered the haze, and there wouldn't be any stopping him until it passed. Ezra never remembered these moments. Often, Ham would have to explain to Ezra what had transpired and fill in the gaps in Ezra's memory. Most of the time, the scenes were gruesome. The first time it happened, Ham described Ezra as a wild animal who had been let loose on an unsuspecting person. While telling the story, Ham had shaken his head in amazement and continued his tale.

"It was pure rage the likes I ain't never seen. It's like you go into some far off place."

When the melee had ended, Ham fired the .38 into the air, and Ezra awoke from his stupor. He still gripped the last of the men by the shirt collar. The man was unconscious, and when Ezra released his grip of the man's shirt collar, the man's body fell to the ground with a satisfying plop. Ham put his hands up and slowly walked toward Ezra.

"Easy," Ham said, "go easy."

Ezra blinked a few times. He recognized Ham, the weapon, and soon he returned from the beyond. Blood dripped from his closed fist. He tilted his head down to appraise his handiwork and inspected his victim: the man's face was so battered, it resembled a month old pumpkin. Ezra stood amidst a pile of contorted bodies. Some moaned in pain. Others were unconscious. Ezra's breathing slowly returned to normal. By the time he sat down in the passenger's seat of their car, he had returned to his old self. After driving down some backroads, he and Ham stopped at a gas station on the way out of town. Ezra found a mirror and was able to clean himself off. He stared at his reflection. His face had changed so much over the years, he could barely recognize himself anymore. He shut his eyes one more time. When he opened them, Ezra was seated at his office desk.

He shuffled the papers around one more time. The new Executive Order was going to give him some restless nights. He wanted to call the reserve branch in the area and tell them to be on the defensive. Someone would try something underhanded, and he was unsure as to how to prevent it. Truthfully, he wanted to be back on the hunt; crack some skulls and track down bootleggers. Instead, he was flying a desk like some waste of space. He looked out the window at the food lines. At least he had a job. He knew he should be thankful for that. But, this situation was not to his liking. Ezra was a man of action. He should be busting up stills, breaking jars of shine, and dropping low-lives. Instead, he was a paper pusher. The more he thought about it, the angrier he got.

The Tracker

OWENS PLAYED WITH THE ENDS OF HIS mustache and tried to ignore his stomach pangs. He craved some Lancashire hotpot, but no place had it. Not to mention, it was easier getting your hand on the sun than some quality russet potatoes. In fact, it was almost impossible to get a decent meal these days. He passed by the crowds milling about in the food lines. Owens himself had probably dropped ten pounds since he'd begun riding the rails, but he had conditioned himself to adapt to the new surroundings. If that meant eating less frequently, among other things, then so be it.

Traveling had become his primary focus, which meant he had to give up on any permanence. He learned how to live out of a suitcase, so to speak. The trains and hotels became his home away from home. He checked his pocket watch. They were due to arrive at the train station in Kansas City in about ten minutes. His stomach growled, but he knew he would have to wait until much later to find some place to eat. He went through his routine of securing his belongings, sat back in the seat, and looked out the window. The blandness of the landscape was comforting in some strange way. It was still a pleasant and calm enough scene no matter how many times he went through the motions. Ultimately, he knew there were worse things than some stomach pangs. Hell, he'd seen many of them up close.

"Excuse me," the lady across from him said. She startled him. She sounded from the Northeast; probably schooled. Her long hair had been pulled back into a bun which sat on the top of her head. She wore gloves even though the temperature didn't call for them. She was classically pretty but not beautiful. She would not have been selected to sit for an artist's portrait, but still, there was something about her to which Owens was immediately attracted.

"Yes," Owens replied.

"Do you happen to have the time?"

Owens reached into his pocket and produced his watch. He flipped it open, and took his time with the gesture. He knew as soon their interaction ended, she would probably leave his company forever.

"It's a few minutes past eight," he said.

She thanked him, and he put his watch away. She sat back in her seat. She was sitting diagonally from him, across the aisle, and was now content to stare out of her window for the duration of the trip. She was probably a school teacher, but Owens didn't know.

Perhaps, in another lifetime he would have been married by now, with children, and it would have been one of his children who would have asked him about the time. Or, maybe it would be his wife who would be the one to ask. The more he considered it, even this woman might have been his wife, had things worked out differently for him. Owens let the fantasy completely envelope him. In his mind, he constructed his house as he thought it would look. He didn't spend too much time on the details of this fantasy, so many of the edges were still frayed. It would be evening time, and he would be in the middle of unwinding from a difficult day at work. He would hear his wife's voice call out to him from the neighboring room.

"Honey, dinner will be ready soon," he imagined his wife would say.

He pictured himself sitting in a comfortable high backed chair in front of a roaring fire. A newspaper would be in one hand, and he'd be holding a tumbler of whiskey in the other. He would have dozed off, but he wouldn't have spilled anything. He would swallow a few times to collect his voice before he replied.

"Sounds good," he would say. Then his mischievous nature would get the better of him and he would add "Would you care to join me for a minute before we dine?"

Owens would hear her footsteps get louder as she approached from the kitchen.

She would pause for a moment in the doorway as if to actually consider his offer. It was the same woman from the train. She would be wearing the same outfit that she was wearing that day, except this time her hair would be unfastened and hang down to her shoulders. He imagined she would blush at his question, but she would regain her composure. She did not answer him. Instead, she took a few steps into the room, so she stood directly behind his chair.

"After dinner," she said.

Though he couldn't see her, he felt her presence behind him. Her warmth radiated from her, even with the heat of the nearby fire. She placed her hands on his shoulders.

"Thank you," he would say. "What are we having for dinner?"

"Lancashire hotpot," she would answer, and she would knead his shoulders with her fingertips.

"You are too good to me," he would say, lean back, and stare at the ceiling. He would continue to tilt his head back until he could see the upside down image of his wife.

"Well, Mr. Owens," she would begin, "it is only because you are so good to me."

She would lean forward and bestow a passionate kiss upon his lips. They would remain embraced for almost thirty-seconds. She would break it off and lean back. He would stand up from the chair and face her.

"Where are the children?" he would ask.

"They're staying with my parents, tonight."

"Smashing."

He would embrace her, and his hands would dance over her body as he caressed her. He would find a slow rhythm even though his heart would be pounding in his chest like the train he knew he must still be riding. Owens would promise not to peek, and she would disrobe before him. He would stay dressed. He could picture her naked without any trouble. Except, for some reason, she still wore those damned gloves. He wanted to continue to indulge the fantasy, but his stomach rumbled again, and he thought about Lancashire hot pot instead. He opened his eyes and was back on the train. He shifted his gaze out the window. They were pulling into the station now.

"Relax," he said to no one in particular.

The train screeched against the rails and slowed down to brake. Owens realized he'd have another minute or so of the trip, and he hoped to recapture some of the previous fantasy. He shut his eyes again. Instead, he flashed back to the European trenches and the sound of incoming projectiles. His wife was gone, and his home had been replaced with the battleground of The Great War.

Even though 1918 seemed like a lifetime ago, Owens could still remember everything clearly. The smell had been overpowering, to say the least, and Owens had marveled at the different kinds of lice he'd found on his body; there had been at least three. The fact he'd managed to stay alive as long as he had, had been a miracle in and of itself; even if he had stopped believing in the existence of God a long time before that.

A few days previous, there had been a gas attack in which he could do nothing to save the lives of the men who'd been unlucky enough to bear the brunt of it. All of his medical training was futile. That particular attack was Phosgene gas. Of course, the effects of the gas didn't register immediately, so most of the men had to face their impending death. Whereas Mustard Gas would burn and blister immediately, Phosgene gas crept along. It would take its time and kill through asphyxiation. The afflicted would experience shortness of breath, which would be the only symptom. Eventually, they would succumb to a pulmonary edema; usually it took hours. As if that wasn't enough, the Jerries would follow it up with a mortar attack. Those lucky enough to avoid a slow death at the hands of the gas might still succumb to a quick death from incoming mortars. This time was no different. Owens heard the high pitched scream of the shells and found what cover he could. He braced himself and listened to the piercing wail of incoming shells followed by explosions. Most of the time, it came down to being able to survive the initial impact or not. At least, a direct hit meant there probably wouldn't be much suffering. A quick death was all most of them prayed for those days, even if they spotted Owens and his medical kit and were in dire need of his services.

After the mortar attack subsided, Owens picked his head up. He was far enough away from the battle to have avoided the barrage, but he could hear the screams from those who were not as lucky. Before he could react, three enemy soldiers came over the top of the trench with bayonets firmly affixed to the ends of their rifles. They had breached the perimeter under cover of the mortar attack, and there was no one left alive to stop them. They jumped from the edge into the trench and charged to attack a cluster of men who'd managed to avoid the primary aerial assault. Owens watched helplessly as the enemy soldiers skewered two allies with their bayonets. They repeated the process three times, each time accompanied by awful screams of men being run through.

When it was over, the enemy soldiers backed away and conversed. They stood in a semi-circle and panted heavily. Then, just as suddenly, they were cut down by a barrage of machine gun fire. Their bodies were practically split in half and collapsed to the ground. Smoke emanated from their wounds and dissipated in the wind. When the sound returned, the wounded friendlies, the few who hadn't been killed, were begging for help. They had been stabbed and repeatedly screamed as much. Owens slithered over to them to see what he could do, but they were beyond help. He could offer them morphine or a bullet, but that was about it. One soldier kept placing his hands over his various wounds in an attempt to stop the bleeding, but he wasn't doing anything worthwhile. Their wounds were beyond the scope of anything Owens could have helped with.

He was a more than capable surgeon; one of the best to ever matriculate at his Alma Mater. He'd saved people who'd been on the brink of death. However, here he was at the mercy of circumstances way beyond anyone's ability. Here, the Grim Reaper was in command and he gave quarter to no one. All things considered, the wounded soldiers lasted longer than Owens would have expected, but they died nonetheless. After the last friendly soldier had passed, Owens heard someone call out to him in English.

"Oy," came from over Owen's shoulder along with the sound of quick footsteps.

"Thank you," Owens said aloud to no one in particular.

A moment went by, and a rail thin Englishman emerged from the shadows. He stopped for a moment, popped out his spent clip from his machine gun, knocked a fresh one against his helmet to align the cartridges, and inserted it into the breech. The man, a Sergeant Louvel, nodded to Owens and took off down the trench. Owens put his head down and tried to block out the world. Then, just as suddenly, as he lifted his head again, he was back on the train.

Since he'd returned from the war, Owens had seen too many shell-shocked soldiers and vowed he wouldn't succumb to the same fate. Sure he would continue to wrestle with his past, but he wouldn't let it win. He continued to stare out the window and without realizing it, he started to grind his teeth. None of this is real he repeated to himself. Soon, the moment passed, and the train pulled into the station.

"Are you alright?" the woman from across the aisle asked. She now stood in the aisle next to his seat. She had looked at him with genuine concern. This episode must have been a bad one, Owens thought. But, he kept it to himself.

"Yes, I'm fine, thank you," Owens replied.

***

The Saloon had technically been out of business since they had begun to enforce the 18th Amendment, but people still congregated there for alcohol. The Weintraub Syndicate had filled the void left by the legitimate bar owners, so the booze never stopped flowing. Most of the furniture had been removed, and pictures no longer decorated the walls, but the chairs were still there, and people occupied them for the time being. No one cared about the decor; they just wanted to satisfy their needs. Years back, some of the windows had been shattered by women involved with the temperance movement, but the windows had long since been repaired. They had remained blacked out, though, so as to keep the current enterprise hidden. Everyone knew it was a speakeasy anyway. However, the law had been paid off, and few raised trouble. The Weintraubs would turn it back into a proper saloon if the eighteenth amendment were repealed. McTavish drank more of his beer. He needed to forget. He hadn't been in the vicinity when the explosion went off, but he'd read the newspaper report, and they had spared no detail. It wasn't his conscience which had weighed on him; he knew that. Still, reading about the details of his exploits troubled him. Remorse: that was probably closer to what he was trying to destroy with booze. He imagined that management would probably be oblivious to the details, and unconcerned with anything except their bottom line. When they had hired him, did they even realize what it was they had truly asked of him when they had asked him to take out the leaders of the labor strike? He put the notion out of his head. Ultimately, it didn't matter. These days, a job was a job; and he needed the money. He had served with some of the board members during the war, and they had remembered his expertise with explosives. One thing led to another, and management recruited him to infiltrate and sabotage the striking labor union from within. The truth was he hadn't rigged any explosives since the war, but that mattered little to those who wanted to rent his services.

The newspaper account of the explosion was horrific, but he knew he would forget in time. He took another healthy pull of his beer. McTavish would tend bar again, one day; probably soon from what he'd heard. If the word on the street was sound, the government would get rid of prohibition, for as much good it turned out to be. He cackled.

"Something funny?" the man seated next to him asked. The man lifted his mug and drained the rest of his glass.

"Just thinking about history," McTavish said. "Name's McTavish," he added and put his hand out to shake. The man stared at it, but only for a second. Then he shook it with enthusiasm.

"Owens," the man replied and started to laugh himself.

"I've got something funny to show you," Owens said and removed a stack of telegrams from his pocket. He placed them on the bar in front of McTavish who read the first telegram.

Taking the train.

McTavish furrowed his brow as if he didn't understand the humor.

"Keep going," Owens said, and gestured McTavish should flip to the next telegram. McTavish flipped through some more.

Still taking the train.

He flipped to another.

Still taking the train.

He kept flipping, but they were all the same.

Still taking the train.

Still taking the train.

Finally, he got to a new one.

Getting off the train.

Walking to the speakeasy.

Look out.

"Huh?" was all McTavish managed. He raised his head out of the telegrams. He hadn't seen the humor. Owens had already stood up and had his Mark 1 Trench Knife in his fist. He bashed McTavish just above the eye and knocked him unconscious. McTavish fell off his stool and lay on the floor. Owens put his knife in its sheath. Afterward, he removed his Colt 1911 and cocked it. He turned around, and met the barrel of a shotgun. It figured a place like this would have protection.

"Wait," Owens said, "I'm a Pinkerton." He nudged

McTavish's body with his foot. "This man is wanted. I'll show you my badge, and the writ."

Owens made a slow move of producing his badge. He kept the Colt pointed at the floor and waited for the bearded man with the double-barrel shotgun to lean in to read the information. The man hesitated for a moment while he made up his mind, but the shotgun never wavered.

"Just don't do nothing in here," the man said.

Owens wanted to say *it's a little late for that*, but he didn't. Instead, he said "No problem. Can you help me move him outside?"

The Preacher

ONOVAN BEGAN HIS SERMON BY SAYING "We are all wicked." Before anyone could object, he continued. "I place myself first in line in that category."

Donovan paused and let the words sink in to placate those who would have openly argued with him. This was not the sort of crowd who kept to themselves, especially if they felt slighted. A few murmurs subsided as people considered what he'd said. He stepped back from the pulpit, so he could see his congregation more clearly. The parishioners were mostly transients, the elderly, and the infirm. No one who sat among the congregation had had a break in the recent past. Since everyone was a hardship case, each of them needed some kind of immediate reprieve. They all looked up at him, in unison, and longed for salvation. The old building creaked as if it were alive and trying to move closer to better listen to Donovan's speech. The church was decrepit and barely held together. Nails protruded from some of the walls, and many of the boards in the roof leaked when it rained. Donovan placed his hands on top of the pulpit and gripped the railings in his hands.

"I ran shine; I cooked it up and sold it."

There was another murmur among the crowd even though the majority of them knew it to be a fact already.

"I am not proud of that, and the Lord struck me down for my wicked ways."

There was a general grumble of acceptance, and then the crowd quieted again.

While they were familiar with his story, most people had waited silently in anticipation and hoped he'd recount the details of his ordeal. It was one of his better sermons, and a favorite amongst the parishioners. Many of his congregation had been with him since the beginning, but they never seemed to tire of hearing him spin this particular tale. At the time of his salvation, when the incident occurred, he had been cooking moonshine. The product had already been created, and now it just needed to be packaged. That evening, Donovan had arrived at his still just as the sun had begun to fade.

The fire he had started now roared. It kept him warm and allowed him to work well in the darkness of night. It was tedious work, but slowly he funneled and dispersed everything into mason jars. Most of these jars would be boxed for transport; steps in the process which were out of his hands. He was only responsible for the manufacturing, and that was fine by him. The Weintraubs paid him well for his work, and he knew his place. Someone else would oversee the transportation. He'd just finished topping off a jar when the dog had come out of the shadows. The wind had picked up as if it had been brought on by the appearance of the animal.

"A tremendous mongrel" Donovan practically yelled to emphasize this part of the sermon. His voice carried above the parishioners, and he startled some of them who had begun to grow weary. He stamped his fists on the pulpit.

"It had red eyes like the devil!" he added.

Donovan remembered the guttural sound which the creature made as it growled. The dog let Donovan know it was close by before it showed itself. He could smell the foul thing from where he stood. They stared at each other in silence for a moment. The dog gnashed his teeth and began to bark. Long threads of saliva dangled from the animal's canines.

"Salvation can be strange and appear before you in

ways you don't expect," Donovan said. He had his congregation in the palm of his hand, and he knew it. They hung on his every word. Donovan paused and made eye contact with as many of them as possible before he continued. He wanted to make sure he didn't lose anyone, though, at this point in the story he doubted he would. Donovan looked down at the eager faces. He closed his eyes. He could almost see the dog before him again. He opened his eyes and looked, once more, on the faces of his congregation.

"I had nothing to save me but the Lord's divine will."

Donovan went back to his memory. On second glance, the beast seemed larger than his initial estimation; perhaps, this was because it was on its haunches now and bristling in an effort to impose itself. Donovan went for his rifle, which was resting against a nearby barrel, but the dog was faster. It snapped at Donovan's neck. He was able to get the stock in the dog's teeth. It clamped down on the rifle, and they shook violently back and forth. Donovan's hands were still cold, and he didn't have a good grip on the weapon. Glass shattered as they careened around and knocked over jars. Donovan tried to hit the animal, but the dog kept its body shifted away, and Donovan's attack did relatively nothing. He couldn't get a shot off either. First, he needed to wrestle the stock out of the dog's mouth, which was not only impossible, but was probably saving his life at that moment.

"The dog could have killed me," Donovan started to say, and his voice broke. He regained his composure and dragged a soiled handkerchief across his forehead. He had begun to sweat; partially from the humidity, but mostly from reliving the vivid memory.

"It was a test," Donovan said.

He remembered how the shadows from the fire had

danced along the ground. The entire time the animal's growls did not stop. Donovan could feel the dog's hot breath on his body.

After tussling around for what seemed like minutes, he finally wrenched the weapon from the dog's mouth. He went to strike the animal with the stock, but it was no use. The rifle was too cumbersome in his hands. It was at that point Donovan first felt his interaction with the dog was supernatural. He sensed something divine may have been at work. Almost as if he were having an out of body experience, Donovan watched as the dog bit him, but he did not feel any pain – that wouldn't set in until later. He didn't know if it was the cold or his adrenalin which staved it off. He was on the ground near the fire. He tried to get up, but he couldn't. The dog could have gone in for the kill, but it didn't. It continued to growl and skulk around the fire for warmth. Then it left just as quickly as it had arrived.

A minute after it was gone, Donovan heard a howl from nearby. The dog had been tracked and cornered by a group of farmers who had picked up the animal's trail earlier and followed. Later, when they retold the story for the hundredth time, the farmers suggested the animal had known the end was near and had accepted its fate. The farmers shot their weapons in unison almost like a firing squad. In his weakened state, and on the verge of death, Donovan had heard the volley of gunshots ring out as the animal met its demise.

"It sounded like judgement day," Donovan said. Now, members of the congregation who had been quietly talking to each other had long since stopped and waited, in rapt attention, for him to continue with his story. Donovan's voice broke again. He hadn't anticipated the rush of emotions, so he took another step away from the pulpit and coughed into his hand. The crowd broke from their trance and some of the more vocal spoke; some stated their approval of Donovan's acceptance of the Lord as his savior. Some questioned the symbolism behind the attack. After putting the dog down, the farmers stumbled upon Donovan's body. Initially, they thought he had been killed. They knew his business operated in the area, and most of the time they would have stayed away except one of them saw the dog's tracks coming from near the still. As they got closer to his body, Donovan began to contort. As the pain set in, he started to moan.

"I felt like I was going to die," he told the congregation.

Of course, he couldn't truly remember what he thought in that moment, but afterward, when he was bedridden, he did indeed think he might die. Plus, it sounded good to be consistent. The farmers had helped him to get home. It was slow going, but they managed to load him into a carriage and drove him back to his house.

As he was placed in his bed, Donovan made a request to one of his cousins, who upon hearing it swore he would take care of everything, which included getting a message to the syndicate. He didn't need to worry about the still. The Weintraubs would deal with it. He was just a cog in the wheel, easily replaced, though they respected his effort and ability.

Donovan passed out soon after. The farmers who'd delivered him had suggested a priest administer last rights. Once word had gotten to the Weintraubs, they sent a physician to look over Donovan while other emissaries tended to the still. They made sure the last shipment of hooch went to transport without further trouble.

Donovan remained bedridden for the following few days. The doctor's forlorn look was burned into his memory, yet another thing he would never forget. The doctor had spectacles, which he untwisted to get out of his pocket and balanced them on the tip of his nose. He looked Donovan over and ran some tests. The doctor's suspicions were confirmed almost immediately, but he waited until he was certain before he broke the news: Donovan had contracted rabies from his encounter with the dog. The symptoms had already begun to manifest themselves.

Donovan didn't know much beyond rumors about the particulars of the disease. The doctor calmly explained the details to Donovan and his family. Donovan would continue to exhibit the following symptoms: excessive salivation, confusion, and anxiety. A Rabies vaccine had been invented, but the doctor didn't have access to it – and in any case, of the twenty-five injections, three needed to be administered on the first day, which had already passed. Donovan asked the doctor about alternative options, but none existed.

"Unless we treat this with the vaccine," the Doctor began to say, but trailed off. He searched for the right words to reassure everyone, but the fact was there hadn't been a single case of anyone surviving the disease without receiving the medicine immediately. All they could do at this point was to make Donovan feel as comfortable as possible and to pray. Donovan thanked the doctor for his time. The doctor had been well compensated by the syndicate, and since there was no more he could do, he was content to be on his way. Donovan made his peace and accepted his fate, whatever that might entail.

Subsequently, he suffered from paralysis and had hallucinations. His kinsmen sat watching him, taking shifts at the end of the bed. During one of his hallucinations, Donovan's grandmother visited. She had been dead for twenty years, but he spoke with her nonetheless. She was still in her burial shroud. She looked the way he'd always remembered her during their limited time together. She was wan with hollowed out features. She spoke in hushed tones, and wore her long hair in a single braid, which rested on one of her shoulders. She stood at the foot of his bed.

"Are you ready to believe?" his grandmother asked.

"Yes," Donovan replied. He was now ready to do anything to be done with the pain and discomfort.

"Who you speakin' with?" Donovan's cousin asked – it was his turn to watch that evening and he sat at the opposite end of the bed. When Donovan answered, the cousin came closer and wiped Donovan's face with a washcloth. Donovan had been running a fever, and sweat clung to his forehead. His cousin had assured him no one was in the room with them, but Donovan could feel his grandmother's presence. When he looked at the foot of his bed, she had vanished, but she visited him a few more times after the initial encounter; she had wisdom to share with him.

"The dog was a message from the Lord for you to change your ways," she said at one point. They were alone in Donovan's bedroom. He was still in the grips of paralysis and a fever, but he understood what she was saying.

"There's still time for you to change," she added.

His grandmother elaborated as to how salvation was still possible for him, if he truly believed. Donovan spent more and more time entertaining her suggestions to become a man of God, and he decided if he survived that was what he would do. He would put his faith in the Lord. The next few days were touch and go. Donovan lost consciousness a few times, and his family worried about whether he would survive. Preparations for his burial were being discussed when the word finally came that he was going to make it. Donovan would become the first man in history to survive contracting rabies without taking the vaccine to combat the disease.

He paused from his sermon yet again. Donovan took his already packed pipe from his jacket pocket, pushed the tobacco with his thumb, and lit the bowl. He blew out a smoke ring.

"I have been saved, and can offer the same for you."

He truly believed what he was saying, but would they?

Donovan looked around from their eager faces to the dilapidation of his church. He extinguished his pipe and placed it on the pulpit. The congregation began to applaud, and though he tried to keep a smile on his face, it disappeared soon afterward.

Toward the end of his sickness, Donovan's kin had advised him to stay in bed, and rest, even after his fever had broken. He couldn't put his finger on it, but something urged him to get out of bed and get to work right away. Perhaps, it was the Lord urging him to get started. So Donovan didn't follow their advice to rest and take it easy. Instead, he renounced his old ways, declared his intentions to start to preach, and sought to break with the syndicate.

When they saw he was serious about his change of conviction, the Weintraubs let him go. He was now a man reborn. It took him a while to find a place to settle down. What little money he had squared away, he spent on the lease to a church. It needed a lot of work to be renovated, and these weren't people who had access to the kind of money he required for the upkeep. By the end of this year, he barely had enough to cover the basic necessities. The church had already been falling apart when he made the purchase, but he was a man of the Lord now and that drive kept him going. Besides, he'd already beaten even worse odds.

The congregation's applause lasted for a few minutes. However, Donovan couldn't help but feel conflicted. His flock was dwindling. Many of these people were just passing through on their way west in search of jobs. If he didn't address the problem, soon the building would be gone; how would he be able to save souls without a church?

The District Attorney

THE DISTRICT ATTORNEY AND HIS WIFE WERE in the middle of having breakfast. Neither of them had gotten out of their robes yet and they were still enjoying the post-sleep haze before the caffeine could take hold. The DA, whose given name was Ezekiel, a name he disliked because people were always shortening it to Zeke, had just finished spreading jam on his toast. He took a bite, and chewed. They were basking in the silence when the phone rang. Laura, the DA's wife, looked at him with imploring eyes. He continued to chew and picked up the phone by the second ring. He didn't even bring it to his ear. Instead, he placed the receiver back down on the cradle and cut the call short. They both laughed, though he knew he might pay hell for it later from his colleagues. Regardless, it made him feel good to relax with her. Even if it only was breakfast, from this point on, he wasn't going to let work disrupt any alone time with his wife. No one was going to take that away from him.

A few years ago, she had been kidnapped, along with her chauffeur. The culprits had held her two days before she was rescued and returned to him. They were holding out for a ransom, to make him drop his most recent case against one of the newly established gangs which seemed to spring up like weeds. To prove they were serious, they had sent her chauffeur back home to deliver their message personally. They had cut out his tongue. The District Attorney had vowed to hunt them down and catch them.

Now, as he watched Laura drink her coffee, he reached out and took her hand in his. He tried to prevent them, but the tears came anyway. It happened less and less frequently these days, although, he would still have breakdowns. He would reassure her they were tears of joy.

The memory was still vivid. After he attended to the chauffeur and got the man to the hospital, he had locked himself in his bedroom and put a plan of action together. He knew the government would grant him help to get her back, but they would only go so far. Everything they did would be done by the book, and every protocol would be obeyed – no matter how devious the perpetrators had been. These people had messed with his family, and they had to pay. He needed retribution. The DA met with his colleagues whose response was lukewarm. Many of them were up for re-election the following year, and no one wanted to do anything to alienate either side of the aisle.

Instead, even while he went through the proper channels, he also put together a team of specialists. He called in every marker, every favor, any currency and goodwill he had ever accrued over the years. Through his connections in law enforcement, he was able to assemble a team of four. Two of them, soldiers who'd seen combat during The Hundred Days Offensive, would keep watch from the outside. The other two, who had had more practical law enforcement experience, would initiate the rescue when the time came. Laura didn't prove be too difficult to track down. They discovered the perpetrators were keeping her captive in a hotel in down-town Kansas City. Later, the same day they had been hired, the four of them created a strike plan. By noon the following day, they were putting it into action. Almost immediately, the rules of engagement they had agreed during preparations went out the window. They had been given assurances from the District Attorney he would handle any fallout from their mission. The way things were going, there was bound to be something.

***

"Gimme a light," Bishop said. It wasn't his given name; they'd all selected names of chess pieces to use. His partner, Knight, didn't respond. Bishop exhaled loudly. He'd already made a fool of himself, or so he thought, when he reached for the matches that he assumed were in his pocket. He'd patted himself down like he was stamping out a fire, before he realized he didn't have them anymore. Bishop pushed his Thompson sub-machine gun over his shoulder, by the strap, so it wouldn't be in his way and asked his partner again.

"Forget about her for a moment," Bishop said when Knight looked over toward the woman on the bed. Bishop was dying for a smoke.

"She's not going anywhere," he added.

Instead of getting up and lighting a match, Knight went back to his paper. Bishop remained calm and placed an unlit cigarette in his mouth.

"Don't make me ask again." Bishop spoke the words with as much anger in his tone as he could muster. The cigarette rose up and down as he spoke.

They were about to begin their second day of watching over the woman, and Bishop felt if he didn't get a chance to smoke, he was going to lose it. Besides, where was she gonna go? All the fight had left her a while ago. Bishop figured he was going to have to teach Knight about respect. After all, he was the senior man here. When he had said 'gimme a light,' it wasn't a suggestion; it was a damned command! As if Knight were suddenly a mind reader, and he knew he'd crossed the line, he slowly got up from the chair, made an overly dramatic gesture of taking the matchbook from his pocket, and approached Bishop. Neither man said anything. Knight struck the match and lit Bishop's cigarette.

"Thank you. Now, was that so hard?" Bishop said and exhaled a cloud of smoke.

Before Knight could answer, both men were spooked by the sound of glass breaking. A split-second later, Knight dropped to his knees and fell to his side. A bullet had caught him center mass in between the shoulders. The District Attorney's wife sat up in bed, alert and frightened, but she didn't try to run. Bishop was in the midst of saying something profound when he was shot too.

"Oh, shi…" he had started to say.

***

Anderson had recited his favorite hymn while he set up his rifle. He and Owens went through their typical repartee and banter the entire time. They'd been engaging in it ever since their induction into the army, and this time was no different.

"You know God doesn't pick sides in this thing, right?" Owens said.

"Stop it; not today," Anderson replied. He fit the sight on top of the barrel and placed the slide on the breech. It was the same conversation, almost word for word, every time. Anderson finished assembling the barrel, stock, and sight.

"You're going to be cold," Owens said.

"I know," Anderson answered.

"Let's get you warm."

Owens read him off some wind readings he'd taken which allowed Anderson to get sighted in with his rifle.

"I see three of them, you?" Owens said after he had looked through a pair of field binoculars.

"Two plus a friendly on the bed," Anderson said.

"Fire, fire, fire," Owens began saying and soon Anderson joined him. They both echoed the words until

Anderson pull the trigger. His M1903 Springfield rifle spat out the projectile. The suppressor muffled the sound of the gunshot, but the glass in the window opposite shattered, and the spent shell flipped out of the breech. It landed on the roof, and Owens' pocketed it. Anderson quickly reloaded and fired again. He hit the second enemy as well. Owens would never admit it, but Anderson was the best rifleman he had ever seen.

They were stationed on the roof of the building adjacent to the hotel. Once the threat was neutralized, both Owens and Anderson dropped to the ground and maneuvered behind the ledge, which would keep them hidden from sight. The sound of the glass breaking had also alerted their benefactor who promptly sent in the assault team. The three of them; the District Attorney, and the two ex-law enforcement agents, were already in the hallway just outside of the hotel room where Laura was being held. With the element of surprise on their side, the melee was over before it began. The ex-law men kicked open the door. The District Attorney went for his wife who, though shocked, had the presence of mind to follow her husband out of the room without commotion. Methodically, the ex-law men made their way through the room. They systematically made sure the two on the floor were dead, putting bullets into their heads to ensure the deed had been done. After all, no one was going to question their methods.

***

"What would you like to do today?" the District Attorney said to his wife as he shook the unpleasant memory from his mind.

"I'm not sure. Let me think about it," she replied.

The District Attorney finished chewing his bread.

Her chauffeur, Liu, showed up he always did during breakfast to see what her schedule would be for the day.

The Chauffeur

L IU WAS IN EXILE FROM HIS HOME. WHEN HE was younger, like many of his acquaintances, he'd gotten involved with gambling as a way to pass the time. It hadn't started out as a problem for him. But, slowly, like quicksand, he had begun to spend more time in the gambling houses and less time focused on his other pursuits. Eventually, the wrong types of people got their hooks into him. He'd fallen behind on some payments for his gambling debts, which resulted in his being targeted by some of the triads. He knew if he didn't settle his debts quickly, which was impossible, it wouldn't be long before they started on his family. He'd heard tales – everyone had – as to what sort of deplorable things they would do to ensure their money was returned. As a measure of last resort, Liu decided to flee the country. He left what meager amount he could, but in the end, he hoped his absence would be enough to appease his usurers and prevent them from taking out their frustrations on his family.

Liu managed to travel to the United States. He'd hidden himself in the hold of a ship, and luckily was able to disembark unseen when the ship had docked in California. He spent a few weeks in San Fransisco's Chinatown, became familiar with the lie of the land, and learned a few key English phrases. He was able to survive due solely to the kindness of a family who had just lost a son around Liu's age. He helped them with chores and indulged their desire of having a complete family, until he felt it was time to strike out on his own. With their blessing, he headed east and eventually settled in Kansas City. Initially, he thought he might continue on to New York City, but he had liked Kansas City, so he decided to stay. Through some divine intervention, or good fortune, he made the acquaintance of the District Attorney and his wife. They had been looking for a chauffeur, someone to accompany Laura during her excursions, and Liu jumped at the opportunity. It wasn't a bad job, and he grew to like and care for his mistress. Mostly, he would escort her places and carry her belongings. When he was not on the clock, Liu would often continue his studies in martial arts; edged weapons were his specialty. Though he hadn't had to prove it yet, he had already become deadly with a blade.

On the day they were kidnapped, Liu had noticed the perpetrators, but he was incapacitated and bound before he could stop them. When he saw the knife, he assumed they were going to cut his bindings. His screams were muffled when they cut out his tongue. They used a branding iron to cauterize the wound, so he wouldn't bleed to death. They told him he should be thankful for that. During the car ride back to the District Attorney's house, while he was unconscious, they placed a list of written demands in his pocket. They barely stopped driving when they pulled over a block away from the house. Someone opened the back door, and pushed Liu out of the car. Liu fell to the ground near the front lawn.

His employers took him to the hospital immediately. The doctor explained to the DA that Liu's physical injuries would heal, but the adjustment to a life without speech would take time. The District Attorney and his wife took care of the medical bills and kept Liu on the payroll. He had thoughts of leaving, but the DA and his wife persuaded him to stay. The bond he had forged with the District Attorney's wife as part of their ordeal was something he couldn't explain. Liu had only ever recognized that type of bond in people who fought in war together. Laura had played the flute in her youth, and she gave one to Liu as a gift. So, rather than live as a mute, Liu used the flute to communicate. It was a rudimentary system, but it worked.

***

The District Attorney hadn't yet gotten over the government's lack of initiative with regard to his wife's kidnapping, when he found he was to be investigated for his role in her rescue. He had made some assumptions about his position within the machine, which had proved incorrect. Not only did he face possible criminal prosecution, but perhaps a civil case as well, if the hotel's management decided to get involved, which they probably would as soon as they smelled blood in the water. Coupled with that was the fact that even though he'd managed to avoid the fallout from the market crash, the residual effects had drained his finances. He'd just gotten off the phone with his accountant. He felt light-headed and sat at his desk. He knew this particular chapter of his life would end soon. He tried to take solace in the fact his wife was safe, but it was overshadowed by his prospective troubles.

The Prisoner

NDERSON HAD A FEW MORE DAYS TO SERVE on the inside, and then he would be free. He'd gone through various stages of throughout his incarceration, and now he realized he was dealing with the final step, and just before it was too late: acceptance. To be honest, he was amazed he'd made it this far. The police, the guards, everyone had tried to break him and get him to cop a plea, but he didn't break. He wasn't the kind of guy who turned. All he wanted, when he was finally released, was to salvage what would be left of this life. He'd had enough of the job.

His cell door slid back and the sound plucked him from his daydream. Two guys he'd never seen before stepped into his cell. They were anglos, and wore prison denim. At first, he was confused as to how they gained access to his cell. However, he figured it out in an instant; the hit was on, and someone with some juice was pulling the strings.

Anderson stood up from off of his bunk and walked to the center of the cell. The first guy, who had blonde hair and a busted nose, took a shiv from behind his back, crossed the room, and tried to stab Anderson in the chest. Anderson could tell by the jerkiness of his movements that the man had had little training with a knife. Anderson took it from him as if they were rehearsing a play and were going to start the scene over. He stabbed Blondie in the kidney, retracted the blade, and drove it into the guy's throat. As this was happening, the second guy, with chin whiskers so black they looked blue, made his play. Anderson let Blondie fall to the ground and turned to face Whiskers. Whiskers knew how to handle a knife, and Anderson was sliced on the forearm. The pain registered as a hot flash, but his adrenalin kept him focused. He hit Whiskers in the stomach; the guy exhaled loudly and backed off. Whiskers sat against the wall and slid down. Anderson took the weapon from Whisker's hand and stuck the point of the blade into his shoulder.

"Tell me who hired you, and I'll call for a guard," Anderson said.

The other prisoner smirked. He wasn't about to become a snitch, and Anderson respected him for that. Anderson stood up and drove his knee into the man's face. Whiskers convulsed as the life fled his body. Anderson sat back down on his bed. It was going to be difficult to explain the two corpses when the next count happened, so he tried to think of more pleasant things.

The Plan

THE DISTRICT ATTORNEY HAD WORKED WITH some of the men before. With the others, he was relying on their desperation to drive them to say yes to his plan. They had the experience to pull off the heist. They just needed to be reminded of the incentive. The DA also needed to convince them it was possible. He had already met with all of them, individually, to gauge their interest and give them some of the details. Donovan needed the money for his church. He and the District Attorney had crossed paths during Donovan's heyday in the bootlegging business.

The previous day, the DA had driven out to the man's church. They had spoken for about twenty-five minutes. Donovan had regaled the DA about his encounter with the dog, and the difficult times he was having keeping his congregation afloat. They also talked briefly about his exploits as a bootlegger. The District Attorney assured Donovan he had no interest in prosecuting him about his criminal history. Rather, it was his experience in this very area which had piqued the DA's interest. It was the sole reason he'd contacted him, now. The DA's pitch was simple. If Donovan joined up, and they were successful, he would never have to worry about money for his church ever again.

Owens had said he would do it for the action. The DA had met him for coffee. They had been at a dry goods store. Migrant workers ambled about. Some of them wore sandwich placards around their necks that explained the details of their current situations. The District Attorney was amazed at the distances some of the men had travelled which had been written on some of the signs. However, he also thought it would help his chances of persuasion should Owens initially decline his offer. He could point to the men wearing sandwich boards and suggest Owens join them in line.

When both of them had arrived, they sat at the table in the front without speaking. They hadn't seen each other since Laura's rescue. They stared at their steaming cups of coffee. Finally, the District Attorney spoke.

"Things are well?" he asked.

"Oh, you know." Owens said and sipped his coffee.

They sat in silence for a moment longer. The District Attorney wasn't going to rush this. Owens was a crucial component to his scheme. When he was ready, the DA went into his pitch. When he had finished, and before Owens could answer, the DA continued to speak.

"Your new job is good?" the DA asked.

"Only thing I was really good at," Owens replied. When the District Attorney didn't say anything further, Owens almost blurted out "Is this thing possible?"

The District Attorney had to smile. The tone of Owen's voice suggested the DA wouldn't have to work very hard to convince him after all.

"If it's done right," the District Attorney said.

***

Ezra had gotten to the dry goods store early. When the DA got to the table, Ezra stood. They shook hands, and both men sat down.

"I had wanted to talk about work," the District Attorney said.

Ezra had furrowed his brow.

"What about?"

The District Attorney had anticipated this was going

to require some finesse on his part, and he was right.

"The gold order," the DA in a whisper.

Ezra exhaled audibly, leaned back, and stared at the ceiling. He wouldn't make eye contact.

"Please tell me you're not thinking about that," Ezra said and continued to look at the ceiling.

The District Attorney changed his tone.

"It solves all of our problems." the District Attorney said and made a shrugging gesture as if to suggest what they were discussing wasn't a big deal. The DA looked at the people who had congregated and formed a line for food. Even if he managed to avoid criminal prosecution, it was only a matter of time before he would have to join the bread lines as well. After all his family had been through already, he wouldn't subject his wife to that.

"If we don't die first," Ezra said.

"Everyone dies at some point," the District Attorney said. "But, this time, we won't," he added.

"Oh, do I have your guarantee, Zeke?" Ezra sat forward and finally looked at the DA. His tone was now openly sarcastic.

When the DA didn't reply, Ezra stood up, stretched, and sat back down. He removed the hat from his head and ran his fingers through his hair. He replaced his hat.

"That's the problem with you dreamers," Ezra said. "You and father were the same way," he added.

Reactions

EZRA LEFT HIS MEETING WITH THE DA AND went directly to the gym.

He hadn't been there in a long time. The place looked to be abandoned, though the equipment still hung from the ceilings. Cobwebs hadn't yet begun to decorate the gear, but Ezra knew that wasn't far off. He settled in and began to hit the heavy bag. The chain which held the bag from the ceiling creaked.

"Who is it?" came from the office in the back.

The voice startled Ezra who thought he was alone. However, he recognized it, which made him feel more comfortable than he would have imagined possible.

"Ezra Cohen," he said.

"Jesus," came the reply.

"No – Ezra,"

"Very funny."

"I thought you was retired?" Ezra said.

Ham came out of the office. He looked like he's been asleep. His hair had begun to go gray, and he stood hunched over. Otherwise, he looked the same; a little beaten down by life, but the same.

"It's good to see you," Ham said.

"I thought I'd hit the bag for a little while," Ezra said.

"You back?" Ham asked. The enthusiasm was now apparent in his voice. He stood up a little straighter as if he'd been jolted with electricity.

"No, just need to let off some steam," Ezra replied. Ham slouched back down and put his hands up.

"Stay as long as you want," he said. Ham went back into the office. He had not done a good job keeping the disappointment out of his voice, but Ezra didn't focus on that now. Instead, he jabbed at the bag and listened to the chain creak some more. Then he got serious.

***

Donovan sat in a pew toward the back of the church and stared at the reproduction of Christ on the cross which hung over the pulpit. He knew it was foolish to wait for a sign. Hadn't he already made up his mind? He looked around the church and listed out loud the various things which needed to be repaired; not to mention that the mortgage on the property would have to be paid off soon, or he would lose it in foreclosure. The wind picked up outside. The fact of the matter was he would probably have to set up shop elsewhere at some point soon anyway. He'd have to say goodbye to this place. And with the money, couldn't he buy a bigger and better church? The more he thought about it, the more he realized he would need to join in with the DA's mission. The church was instrumental. In that moment, he realized he'd already made up his mind. He wouldn't need to wait for a sign.

***

Anderson heard the footfalls in the hallway. Two people were approaching his cell.

Was it going to be another attempt to end his life? Maybe. Even though they had failed, it wasn't like them to send another envoy so soon, although, times could be changing. Not to mention, he didn't know which faction had wanted him rubbed out. It could be multiple. The eye cover slid back. Anderson couldn't tell who was at the door.

"Get your things," the voice said. The man stayed

behind the door and spoke through the partition.

"Don't have any," Anderson replied.

"Alright."

The door opened and a guard came into the room. His night stick was outstretched. He gestured with it for Anderson to back against the wall next to the cot. Another guard entered the room, similarly armed, with his truncheon ready. So, this was going to be it. They had paid off the guards, and now Anderson was going to get tenderized like a side of beef. Both guards were on the younger side. They didn't look like they had had much experience, and the fear was palpable in both of their eyes. Still, it wasn't something Anderson looked forward to dealing with.

"What's the rumpus?" Anderson finally said.

"You're being released."

***

The next day, all of the perspective crew members assembled in the District Attorney's kitchen. Each of them had signed on for the mission. The District Attorney's wife would be out for the day which left them some time to plan and iron out the rest of the details of the heist. The men sat around the dining room table. The District Attorney stood at the head, ready to begin the discussion, when someone knocked on the door. It captured everyone's attention. The DA went to see who it was, conversed with the person for a moment, and put his John Hancock on a form. He walked back inside to the kitchen, and Anderson followed him.

***

Anderson was more chiseled than Owens remembered, but it was him.

He had the same face. It was just sharper in some ways. It looked like he'd lost some hair and some weight. Anderson spotted an empty seat by Owens and occupied it. The two men shook hands and intimated they would catch up after the meeting.

"Gentlemen," the District Attorney began and made sure to have everyone's attention before he continued.

"In April, President Roosevelt signed Executive Order 6102 which made it a federal crime to horde gold. If you are found guilty, it's a $10,000 fine, or you can be sentenced to two years' imprisonment, under the Trading with the Enemy Act of 1917. Therefore, gold must be warehoused for the duration of the order. The government will store this gold at the Federal Reserve bank here in Kansas City, and offer a flat fee of 20.67 per ounce."

He paused.

"We will rob one of the more high profiled jewelers when he goes to make his deposit." He paused again and tried to make the end of his speech sound like it would be easy. "We will accost him, collect the gold, and be on our way."

The District Attorney waited again; this time, for them to process the information. He didn't expect it to take long, since he had already explained many of the details to them when they had met individually. Now, as a group, there was still no immediate dissent.

"I'll step out for a moment, so you can think it over," the DA said and walked toward a side door. He gripped the handle and faced them once more. "If any of you have any last second hesitations, now would be the time to bring them up." He stopped speaking and stepped into an adjoining room.

Once he departed, the room stayed quiet. No one said anything for a moment. Finally, Owens spoke. "So, what do you think?"

Liu, who was standing in the back, picked up his flute and played a trill of notes.

"What does that mean?" Owens said. He turned around in his seat and looked from Liu back to the rest of the group.

"I think it means, he's in," said Ezra. He was seated at the opposite end of the table.

Owens shook his head in agreement as if Ezra's analysis was acceptable.

"Okay," Owens said. He jutted his chin toward another of the men he had just been introduced to and said "What about you?"

Donovan hesitated before answering. "I think I'm in, too."

"You think?" Owens asked. His tone was aggressive.

"I need the money," Donovan replied. His own tone had become aggressive as well.

"What about you?" Ezra asked Owens.

"I made my decision yesterday."

Preparations

THAT NIGHT, AFTER ALL OF THEM HAD agreed to participate, each man returned home to steel himself for the challenge which lay ahead. Everyone had a specific role, but to pull this thing off they would have to work together in harmony like an engine firing properly on all cylinders.

Liu returned to his room within the DA's house. He had already reconciled the possibility he might not return from this mission. Regardless, he owed the District Attorney. Liu had gone over his situation in the kidnapping hundreds of times, looking to place blame and find fault with someone, anyone, but ultimately it didn't matter. He knew events in one's life lined up in a linear way in retrospect, but it was a chaotic jumble as one went through it all. The fact remained: by making sure he was immediately hospitalized, the District Attorney had most likely saved his life. Liu realized he owed the DA alone for that. Examining the past might reveal new insight, but it wouldn't help him with his current situation. The only acceptable move to pay anything back was to go forward and make the most of this opportunity. He picked up his flute and played a few notes. Liu had come up with a basic system of playing certain trills for "yes" and others for "no." The majority of the time, however, he was happy to remain silent and just listen.

He would serve as the distraction for the heist. He would act as a music performer who had been separated from his group and didn't speak English. He would stop the vehicles a block away just after they had entered the field of fire. He would also be responsible for taking out as many as possible of any guards who attended the jeweler. There might be as many as eight people in total.

A gun would have been the best resource to have, but the sound would alert those within earshot, and the crew needed time before there was a shoot-out. Even though the DA's team would try to provide for minimal casualties and destruction, each of them knew that the bullets would begin to fly once the melee started. Too many trigger happy people were in the mix for that not to be the case. Liu attached a knife blade to the end of the flute and began to weld it. When he was finished, he tested his work. The blade on the end of the flute made a slight noise as it cut through the air. This would work for him.

***

Ezra was already beginning to suck wind, and it hadn't even been three rounds.

He'd warmed up a bit, shadowboxed, and figured he'd get a few rounds in on the heavy bag. For a few days now, he'd been coming to the gym after hours to let off some steam. Ham had told him to do what he needed and to lock up before he left. It was only at that point Ezra realized that Ham had been living at the office. Times were indeed tough, and it only served to give Ezra more fuel. If the take was big enough, he could help Ham with some of his financial woes. While Ezra was doing reasonably well, as compared to others, he knew it was only borrowed time.

He unleashed another combination on the bag and took a few deep breaths. It burned his lungs. At first, when they had discussed Ezra's role in the plan, he was going to be the inside man responsible for passing information along and keeping an ear on the proverbial grapevine. However, he had balked against simply being what he thought of as a messenger. He wanted to get his hands dirty. His punches seemed to be in rhythm with his thoughts, and he thudded the bag with crippling shots as he forced the anger back. He couldn't afford to have a dissociative episode now, so he stepped away from the heavy bag and calmed himself. In the end, he had agreed to provide inside information, and keep tabs, if he could also be on one of the teams which took the jeweler.

"I need to be in the mix," he had said.

When his partners had seen the look in his eye, no one had opposed him. He would be part of the second wave of the attack along with the preacher. Ezra somehow felt pacified by these thoughts and resumed his workout. Even though he still needed to develop his conditioning, his combinations felt crisp.

***

Donovan knelt down in the pew directly in front of the statue of a crucified Christ and he tried his best not to audibly moan as he prayed. He had been at it for about forty-five minutes. He hoped this time, there would be a sign or some sort of reassurance he was doing the right thing. Before they committed the heist, their group would have all the information they would need, and everything would be meticulously planned. However, if Donovan knew anything for certain, it was that nothing ever went strictly according to plan. He had told himself he would be breaking the law for a noble cause. He was not going to return to a life of crime. This was going to be a one-time thing, which he was doing for the benefit of his congregation. Didn't they all deserve a chance at salvation? Was he not the agent to bring about that change? He racked his brain for any biblical examples to make himself feel less guilty, but he had trouble thinking of anything.

***

Anderson tilted back the whiskey.

It had been a long time since he'd had any booze, and he savored it. He swished it around in his mouth before he swallowed. He and Owens were at a speakeasy. It happened to be the same one from Owens' earlier exploits in which he'd tracked down and arrested the Irish explosives expert. However, the word on the street was prohibition would be repealed any day now. It was only a matter of time. Both of them had sensed this might be one of their last times to whet their proverbial whistles together, so when Owens suggested they catch up over a beverage, Anderson had jumped at the chance. During the heist, they were going to take over watch from across the street; partnered up again like the old times. Before he'd killed the first drink, Owens had already regaled Anderson with the details of his life as a Pinkerton Agent. Mostly, he travelled around and arrested thieves and saboteurs for the railroad, but he was more curious about Anderson.

"So, what the hell happened to you?" he finally said after talking non-stop for a few minutes straight.

Anderson stared at the lip of his drink.

"Well," he began and launched into his history over the last few years.

After they had finished rescuing the District Attorney's wife, Laura, Anderson had worked as a mercenary. He had grown accustomed to the action, and during his downtime he started to get reckless as a result. Bootlegging had grown in popularity, and it had given him the opportunity to find work for various factions.

"It must have taken his final chit to spring me from prison," Anderson said in reference to the District Attorney.

"Anyway," he began again and went back to telling his story.

During a raid, he had been arrested, and the powers that be sought the maximum term possible. Every syndicate was worried about Anderson's allegiance, and at one point they tried to silence him permanently. Even after an attempted assassination, however, Anderson continued to keep his mouth shut. His code prevented him from becoming a snitch and giving in to the prosecutor's demands.

"Lord knows they offered me almost anything I could have wanted."

In the end, he was content to do his time and let fate handle everything. So, he kept to himself and didn't play ball. No matter what offers he received, he turned them down. This was the life he had chosen. He continued to do his time quietly until the District Attorney had him released.

"That about sums it up," Anderson said. He had always been a man of few words, and this time was no different. They were diametric opposites of each other, Anderson and Owens. It was probably the main reason why they functioned so well as a team. They ordered another round and continued to drink well into the evening.

The District Attorney's Wife

THE DISTRICT ATTORNEY AND HIS WIFE HAD finished dinner. They were in the middle of desert. Though it had been a pleasant evening, neither of them felt much like indulging in conversation. Laura had grown accustomed to life again after her kidnapping, and while she had become a somewhat different person, the vibrancy of her former self still shone through. However, it was going to be a difficult few days ahead for both of them. They had agreed she should stay with her sister in New York for the next few days. This was necessary but it would take its toll since she and her sister had been quite estranged for the last few years. Regardless, Laura would take the first train the next morning. Later, the District Attorney would meet up with her, and from there they would board a ship to South America. Both of them realized they might not be able to return to America for a while, if ever.

The Federal Reserve Bank

9 **25 GRAND STREET OFFICIALLY OPENED IN 1921.** It was the headquarters of the Federal Reserve. The building was enormous, with twenty-one floors. It could be seen from miles around. At one point, it held the record for being the tallest building in Kansas City. The District Attorney had been able to rent an office from the bank. It made sense to him to hide in plain sight. That morning, the men loaded their gear into duffel bags, donned painting attire, and entered the building. If anyone saw them, they would appear to be a work crew out to do some renovating.

Except for Anderson and Owens who would be stationed across the street, the rest of the men assembled in the empty office. The District Attorney's bankroll had been depleted to pay the rent for the next month, but when they succeeded it would all be worth it. The Jeweler had planned on making his drop off during a holiday, which would help to limit the amount of people on the street. The DA's crew would also ensure few people would be on the street when the heist went down. They continued to set everything up well into the evening, when Ezra arrived with some bad news for the group.

Earlier in the year, in what would became known as The Kansas City Massacre, four law enforcement agents had been killed by a gang led by Vernon Miller, which included Charles 'Pretty Boy' Floyd. The operation was to free Frank 'Jelly' Nash from custody before he could be returned to Leavenworth penitentiary. As a result of this and an increase in organized criminal activity, the Bureau of Investigation was now operating as The Division of Investigation, and would be another enterprise on which Ezra needed to keep tabs and provide disinformation. However, while they all realized it might become a problem, it didn't change anyone's disposition toward going through with the heist. As far as everyone was concerned, the plan was still going forward.

The Jeweler

ORDECAI BENEDICT'S FATHER HAD BEEN a jeweler. It was how Mordecai got started in the business: he worked for his father. In the beginning, when he was still a child, he would sweep up, carry boxes, and set up display cases. Over time, he got involved in sales and helped to promote the business until it was thriving. When his father, Hyman, retired, Mordecai took over the day to day operations. He saw no reason to reinvent the wheel, but he helped expand the company to invest in gold and other precious metals. He had missed the gold rush of the previous century, but he saw the potential so he invested the majority of his wealth into the accumulation of precious metals. Even during the tumultuous times of the last few months, things had been going well. Mordecai was never one for stock speculation, so he had avoided the crash.

Now, however, with this new edict, he was going to have to relinquish 150 kilograms of gold. True he would have certificates of ownership, and be compensated, but he hated having to part with any of the merchandise. He figured he would hire some bodyguards to make sure he was protected during and after the delivery. Not that he didn't have faith in the government, but these days, it paid to be shrewd.

The Day

"HOW MUCH DID HE SAY, AGAIN?" OWENS said.

He and Anderson had set up on the roof top a block away from The Reserve Building. Their target was scheduled to make his deposit in about a half an hour. So far, Ezra's intelligence had been perfect.

"One hundred and fifty kilograms," Anderson said.

He had already assembled his rifle and was looking through the sight at the various incoming cars down on the street. The other teams would place the road closed signs in a few minutes

"How much is that?" Owens said.

Whether he knew the answers already and was going into his routine remained to be seen.

"It's thirty-three dollars an ounce, and there are thirty-five ounces in a kilogram," Anderson said. He knew what Owens had wanted to hear him say, but he figured he'd drag their conversation out a little and not indulge him right away.

"How much is that?" Owens said, again.

He had repeated his question word for word with the exact same tone he'd had before.

"It's roughly one hundred seventy-five thousand dollars."

"How much is that split four ways?"

"There are five of us."

Without missing a beat, Owens asked another question.

"How much is that split five ways?"

"It's about thirty-five grand a piece."

"You could buy an island with that," Owens said.

The statement was matter-of-fact, as if he was pointing out something obvious. Neither man spoke for another minute.

"What are you going to do with your share?" Owens said.

"Assuming we make it out of this?" Anderson replied.

"What are you going to do with your share?" Owens said.

Once more, he repeated the question with no change to his tone. The truth was Anderson hadn't thought about it. He never thought about the future. He wanted to stay focused on the task, and he believed if he contemplated the details of the future, it would prove to be a distraction.

"It depends," Anderson said.

"What are you going to do with your share?" Owens said a third time.

"Maybe buy a spread somewhere," Anderson said. "You?"

"I'll probably buy that island," Owens said.

***

Ezra paced back and forth. He always got antsy before a fight, and today had been no different.

He checked the time. The Jeweler had scheduled his deposit for about a half an hour from now. Ezra continued to shadowbox for a moment. He could feel the fugue state lurking, like an animal waiting to pounce, but he wanted to time it to coincide with the arrival of the jeweler.

"Are you a man of God?" Donovan asked.

They had been standing on the street corner a block away from the reserve. While Ezra paced the sidewalk,

Donovan rested against a building and smoked his pipe. Ezra stopped walking. He lifted his head to look up to the heavens as if he was looking for confirmation from the Lord.

"Ha," Ezra said and resumed his pacing.

***

Liu's dream the night before included too many symbols and omens which signified his death. However, he felt strangely at peace with the approaching doom. Liu had come a long way since his days in the gambling houses. He thought back to his youthful stubbornness and wondered how his family might be doing. He debated as to whether any retribution had been visited upon them by the triads in his absence. He felt ashamed for how selfish he had been. The opportunity for him to write his family a letter had always been there, but he could never bring himself to do it. These days, he tried to imagine they didn't exist anymore, and for a while he was able to believe it; but recently, memories of them wouldn't be denied.

Earlier in the morning, Liu had stood in front of the full length mirror in his room in and marveled at how much he had resembled his father. He was dressed in some traditional Chinese attire to better simulate the ruse he would have to enact later in the morning. He brought the flute to his lips and played a trill. Liu realized he could more than make up for his selfishness during today's excursion. Now, he waited patiently on the street corner, glad of his opportunity to help the DA and his wife, and excited he had a chance for penance.

***

All morning, the DA had thought about everything he would

no longer be able to do after the next few hours had passed; restaurants at which he could never dine again, people he could never speak with. Similarly, he thought about Murphy's Law: how anything which could go wrong *would* go wrong. The fact that any of his crew might be killed weighed heavily on him. He wasn't going to put himself in harm's way today. He was able to avoid any carnage simply because he had bankrolled everything and used his connections. Really, though, was what his partners were about to do the true measure of a man? Not to mention, their success could come down to something as whimsical as Benedict deciding he would make his deposit the following day. The DA commanded himself to stop thinking about things so negatively, but it was impossible.

***

Benedict had hired the bodyguards against the advice of his wife, brother, and sister-in-law. They thought it would be a waste of money.

"Who in their right mind would rob a federal reserve deposit?" they said.

"Desperate people," Morty replied.

He had already made his decision, so once he knew the date he was going to make the deposit, he hired five bodyguards to accompany him. They all had some form of law enforcement or military experience, and they were more than happy for the chance to work. It may have been overkill, but he'd been successful this far in life by being a cautious contrarian. When someone told him not to do something, he instinctively did it anyway. Usually, it worked to his benefit. When his business associates had suggested he invest in the stock market, he had said no. When a family member had tried to dissuade him from spending his money on investing in precious metals, he politely heard them out then spent his money anyway. It was one of the surest ways he knew how to make money: always bet against the tide. So, that morning, he'd had the men load the gold into the second of two cars. He would ride in that car with two of them in the front seat. The other three bodyguards would be in the first car. They would ride ahead and scout for trouble; not that there was likely to be any, but again, it paid to be cautious.

The second car was a few lengths back when Morty and his two companions witnessed someone approach the first car as it stopped at the corner between 8th and 9th street; about a block away from The Reserve Bank. The man wore some sort of traditional Chinese garb and carried a flute.

***

Liu made it to the window of the first car. He didn't know if the gold would be in the first or the second, but that wasn't his job to find out. He was just supposed to distract the first car, so the second car could catch up and enter the line of fire.

"Help you, chief?" the driver asked.

Liu stared at the man for a moment.

"Maybe he don't understand no English," Liu heard from the back seat. Two men had ridden up front, with a third one in back. Liu brought the flute to his lips and started playing.

"Oh, Christ," said driver. "Hey, listen pal, we gotta get going," the man added.

He was a compact man wearing a peaky hat. He had thick scar which ran across his forehead and fractured one of his eyebrows. Liu continued to play.

"Come on, let's go," came from the back seat.

Liu looked out of the corner of his eye and saw the second car approach. He stopped playing. This would be his chance. While the men in the car might have superior firepower, Liu had the element of surprise and he wasn't in a confined space.

"Great, now get the hell out of here!" the driver said.

Liu bowed slightly. The second car had pulled in a few lengths back from the first. Liu turned his flute around and jabbed the driver in the side of the neck with the knife blade.

***

"Murder!" the man in the back seat screamed. The interior of the car was sprayed with arterial blood when the Chinaman removed the blade.

The driver flailed about and gripped at the wound. He tried to stop the blood flow, and press down on the gas pedal, but somehow his foot wouldn't work.

"Get out of here!" the man in the backseat yelled.

The Chinaman was able to hit the driver again, this time in the face. The blade pierced the man's cheek, and he vomited blood and bile. He withdrew the weapon once more and the driver fell to his side. The man in the back seat continued to scream, and the Chinaman ducked down so he would be out of their line of sight. He ambled to the back door, walking along on his knees then popped up quickly and tried to break the backseat window with the blunt end of his flute. He'd gotten one good crack at it and dropped back down. The man in the back seat started to moan. The Chinaman waited another moment and jumped up again to strike the window when bullets from a Thompson machine gun hit him in the chest and blew him off his feet. The man in the front passenger seat, who hadn't spoken the entire time, had fired his weapon.

He shattered the rear door's window, and the sound from firing his weapon inside made his ears ring. Eventually sound filtered back into the car. He kept the weapon raised off of his lap as the barrel was still hot. Smoke continued to emit from the nozzle. Both passengers looked out the open window; the Chinaman had not moved since he'd been hit. The projectiles had probably killed him on impact.

***

The driver would die. Of that much, Liu had been almost certain. He had most likely severed the man's carotid artery with the first blow. However, the man continued to thrash about, and Liu wanted to make certain, so he had gone for a follow-up shot. The man in the back seat had screamed repeatedly which was what drew Liu's focus. Perhaps this was the man who was guarding the gold.

Liu had a choice; he could either flee and reset for another assault, or he could push his luck. The element of surprise was clearly gone, and he knew he'd be chancing it if he attacked the man in the backseat. But his adrenaline had compromised his logic. He decided to continue his assault and went for the back window. The glass held out on the first strike, although it had begun to crack and a spider's web of shards were now visible. He was going to go for a second attempt when bullets fired from the man in the passenger seat shot out the window and took him in the chest. The pain was unlike anything he had ever experienced, but it didn't last long. He didn't even have time to think about how unfortunate he'd been to tempt fate a final time. He was dead before he had hit the ground.

***

"What the hell are they doing up there?"

The men in the second car had pulled a few lengths behind the first car and watched with curiosity as a musician, decked out what looked like pajamas, played the flute next to the driver's window.

"What do you think?" the man in the passenger seat had said. His name was Franklin. He'd been a decorated soldier in the Great War but had suffered from what doctors were calling "War Neurosis." Every so often he would repeat the same questions, and on occasion exhibit verbal tics or make noises of which he was unaware. It had been disconcerting at first, but his mastery of a Steyr, which he'd pilfered off of a dead German soldier, was unparalleled, so if it meant tolerating some outburst every so often that was fine by Morty. Almost on cue, Franklin emitted a noise similar to the squeak of a mouse. The driver didn't respond. He'd grown accustomed to it as they all had.

"On any other day, I'd think nothing of it," Morty began "But, it seems like more than a coincidence, doesn't it?"

"What does that mean?" Franklin said.

It was another thing Morty appreciated about the man; he was honest, even if he wasn't the brightest. Most people would have just agreed with Morty about it being coincidental, even if they hadn't known what the man had meant.

"It's strange something so odd happening on the same day we're making this delivery."

Franklin nodded his head in understanding. The silence which accompanied his revelation was shattered by the sound of machine gun fire. The source came from the first car, and the projectiles had nearly cut the Chinaman in half. Morty let out a series of profanities at the validation of his suspicion, and he looked around to see if he would be under attack as well.

"Go!" Morty commanded the driver, who pressed on the accelerator and the car shot forward. The man in the passenger seat cradled a Tommy Gun in his lap and emitted another squeak as the car gained in speed.

***

From their elevated position on the roof across the way, Anderson and Owens watched as Liu took almost a full clip of bullets to the chest. The sound was delayed, so Liu had collapsed to the ground silently. A moment later, the sound of the bullets reached them; it sounded like a jackhammer hard at work. Neither man said anything. They had seen too many of their colleagues die, though they would drink to Liu that evening should they emerge victorious.

"Think you can take out the tires from here?" Owens said.

"Yes," Anderson replied.

"I'm not sure; that's a pretty long ways away."

Both men knew Anderson had made longer shots before under worse circumstances. Anderson calmed his breathing and sighted his rifle on the second car's front left tire. When he saw Anderson undergo the start of his ritual, Owens began to chant the word fire softly over and over again. Anderson squeezed off a shot. He didn't use the suppressor this time, since there was no need to mask their direction. The weapon fired, and a beat went by. Then, the front tire exploded and the car sagged on its rim.

"Nice shot," Owens said.

"Thank you," Anderson began and followed with "I'll add it to your tab."

Both men ducked down behind the ledge when the

men below opened fire at them.

***

The gold had been converted into 12.5 KG bars, and there were 12 of them. Each bar weighed close to twenty-eight pounds, so they had been split into 6 groups of 2, which had each been placed in burlap flour sacks. These were the only bags which had enough tensile strength to transport them.

"Out of the car," Franklin said.

He rolled down his window and leaned the top half of his body out so he had a better trajectory with his weapon. He fired the Thompson toward the roof of the building across the way. The men in the first car had already dispersed and were firing at the roof too. All of them had crouched down behind the trunk or hood and kept the car's chassis in between them and the building.

Morty climbed out the other side. He hesitated and reached for a sack.

"Just go; it'll be fine," Franklin said, as if he could read Morty's mind.

Franklin changed out a clip and opened fire as Morty exited the vehicle. Both Franklin and his colleague waited for their compatriots from the first car to open fire at the roof before they emerged from the car.

***

Ezra and Donovan had waited for Benedict and his crew to drive past the point of no return and into the zone of fire. Afterward, they put phase one of the plan into motion. They arranged some 'Road Closed' signs in the middle of the street where Grand Boulevard intersected first with 8th street and then at 9th street. Once they finished with the signs, they distributed Caltrops, antipersonnel weapons, which they scattered about the street on either side of the signs. If and when the authorities were alerted by the gunfire and tried to intervene, the tires of their cars would be destroyed by the Caltrops. Once they were done, both Donovan and Ezra took refuge in a storefront near the melee and readied themselves for the upcoming battle.

Ezra felt the fugue state envelope him like an ocean wave. While he had been strenuously keeping the feeling at bay earlier, once the bullets started flying he welcomed it like an old friend. Soon he was completely under the hypnotic spell. The fear didn't disappear, but he wasn't bothered by it. Death was no longer a frightening prospect, and he realized he was ready to join the fray. Donovan had continued to pray since he and Ezra had hidden themselves in the entryway of the building half a block away. He did it silently at first, and then when he heard gunshots he became vocal. He didn't care whether his partner found his praying to be bothersome; the time for courtesy had long since evaporated. Donovan looked to see how Ezra would react, but the man had undergone some sort of transformation. A strange look was plastered on his face, and his eyes were wild.

"Amen," Donovan said as he finished a prayer. He racked the shotgun, and the noise caused Ezra to momentarily break from his trance.

"Ready to earn our money?" Donovan asked. Both of them rolled out and headed toward the parked cars.

***

Owens scanned the street with his binoculars and saw Ezra and Donovan sprint toward the convoy.

"We need some cover fire," Owens said calmly.

Anderson squeezed off two shots which skimmed

the trunk of the first car and the hood of the second. Their targets had been doing a good job of staying hidden, but Anderson figured Donovan and Ezra should be able to flush them out like game or possibly take care of everything on their own. Anderson swept his rifle over the field of fire. A shot sounded from behind them on the roof and the bullet hit Anderson. He dropped the rifle, which plummeted down the side of the building.

He fell onto his side and lay motionless. Owens had already produced his Colt, and he faced the man who had fired the bullet. They had their weapons pointed at each other.

"Don't even think about it," the man said to Owens.

***

Franklin realized he hadn't made a squeaking noise since the gunfire had started. Perhaps it was connected, but he didn't stop to think about it. He'd placed the Thompson on the street by his feet; he'd run out of ammunition. While there were more clips in the car, he had another idea. As he tried to remain hidden behind the car, he reached above him and ripped the side mirror off the chassis. He angled it to be able to look at the roof. With his free left hand, he removed his Steyr from its holster. He yelled out and got the attention of the bodyguard by the trunk of the first car.

"Cover me," he yelled.

Simultaneously, all of them opened fire toward the roof. Franklin waited a moment then took off toward the entrance of the building. He'd dropped the mirror, but the Steyr was outstretched in his right hand. Luckily, his conditioning was still good. He took the stairs two at a time, and before long he had made it to the roof. He silently opened the door and saw two men lying down by the roof's ledge: a sniper and his spotter. Franklin quietly shut the door behind him, walked to within range, and fired his Steyr. He hit the sniper in the back. The man dropped his weapon and fell to the ground. The spotter was quick and had already produced his weapon before Franklin could squeeze off another shot.

***

"So, what do we do now?" Owens asked.

"That's a great question," the man said and looked like he was actually giving it consideration. He grimaced in concentration, but the gun never wavered.

"Why don't both put down our weapons until we figure this out?" Owens said.

"Okay," the man replied.

Both of them hesitated. Neither wanted to drop his gun before the other one had. They needed to do it at the same time. Once they found the rhythm, each of them delicately laid their weapons by their feet.

"Why don't—" the man began to say, but Owens had already slipped the knuckle duster of his Mark 1 Trench knife on his fingers and closed the distance between the two of them.

***

Owens couldn't believe his luck in having to deal with such a simpleton. He stuck the man in the stomach with the knife. The man let out a sound similar to a bellows closing, and then some sort of high pitched squeak. Owens ripped the blade north and spilled the man's innards onto the rooftop.

"But—" the man had begun to say before he collapsed. While on the ground, he lived long enough to try and shove his entrails back into his body. He was unsuccessful and died soon after.

***

Owens wiped the knife blade on the man's shirt and ran over to check on his partner. Anderson was unconscious, with shallow breathing, but he was still alive. It had been a long time since Owens had practiced medicine, but there weren't any alternatives. It didn't appear to have hit any major organs, and unless the bullet had nicked the brachial artery, Anderson would live. But Owens would need to be certain. Plus, if he didn't at least clean the wound and remove the projectile, Anderson might succumb to sepsis.

Owens didn't have any equipment with him except for his trench knife, so that would have to do. Anderson was already unconscious, so Owens maneuvered him away from the roof's edge. He used the knife to cut Anderson's shirt away, and mopped up as much of the blood as he could. Following that, he took the hip flask from his pocket, disinfected the knife blade, and poured the remnants of it on the wound. Beneath him came the sound of continuous gunfire, and the screams of men who'd been shot or stabbed. Owens did his best to block out the sound of carnage and began to perform surgery on his friend.

***

There were four of them remaining; Benedict and three of his bodyguards. The bodyguards continued to fire off rounds at the roof even though there hadn't been any return fire for the last few minutes. Ezra and Donovan waited for the last fusillade to stop. They opened fire on both cars. They shattered the window glass and put a series of holes in the chassis of both cars. Donovan was stealthy; he peeked around the corner, opened fire, and hid behind the building facade on the corner. Ezra was a little more reckless. He left the confines of the building and ran toward the second car in a zig-zag manner. He drew the bodyguard's gunfire away from the roof, and though he took a slug for his effort, it didn't seem to faze him. He rounded the trunk of the second car and opened fire on the first bodyguard he saw. Ezra shot him multiple times.

Donovan emerged from the behind his cover and fired his shotgun at the first car. He dropped the gun, and took out a jar which had been filled with shine. A soaked cloth peeked out from underneath the lid. Donovan lighted the end of the cloth and hurled it toward the car. He had wanted to watch the incendiary weapon arc through the sky and shatter on the trunk, but he valued his life more, so he ran back to the safety of the building facade just before the enemy opened fire on him. However, his aim had been true, and the jar exploded on the trunk of the first car. The flaming liquid splashed off every side and dowsed one of the bodyguards who'd been hiding by the trunk of the car. He immediately went up in flames, screamed, and flailed about. He took off running like he could somehow escape the pain and made it about twenty feet before he pitched over, dead.

***

Ezra was still deep in the clutches of his fugue state. He knew he'd been shot, but he hadn't felt any pain. It was one of the benefits of being immersed in this haze. He heard screams, and smelled something cooking. It had been similar to the smell of bar-b-que. He had started to think about a joint he loved near the office, but he put the thought from his head. Ezra was about to return to the safety of the building on the corner, when he spotted a man cowering near the front of the second car. The man was well dressed but looked soft and doughy. He had to be Benedict. Ezra sprinted toward him. Benedict heard the approaching footfalls, even above all of the commotion, and tried to run, but Ezra tackled him. He rolled the man onto his back.

"Please—" was all Benedict could get out. Ezra had already begun to pummel the man's face. Benedict stopped speaking after the first punch. He stopped moving after the second. Ezra had probably broken most of the bones in Benedict's face after the fourth punch. Ezra would have continued to administer the beating, but he was shot in the head.

***

Donovan had tried to warn Ezra of the remaining bodyguard, but it was almost as if Ezra had gone deaf. He had already beaten their enemy to death, yet he continued to punch the corpse. Ezra's obliviousness gave the final bodyguard enough time to line up an easy shot. Donovan would have fired the shotgun, to distract the man, but his vision was partially obscured by the smoke. After the man had shot Ezra, Donovan left the safety of the building, crossed into the middle of the road, and shot the final bodyguard.

Although it seemed like the gunfight had raged for hours, it had probably only gone on for ten minutes. The police had tried to enter into the action, but the caltrops had worked, and deterred any outside intervention. Donovan went to check for a pulse on Ezra's body but couldn't find one. Soon afterward, a car pulled up alongside him. It had been parked across the street, and while it had suffered some minor damage, it would be more than adequate for their purposes. The DA was behind the wheel. He and Donovan nodded to each other. The DA exited the vehicle and left the motor running. Both he and Donovan checked that none of the bodyguards had survived. The final bodyguard, who had killed Ezra, had only been wounded by Donovan's bullet. He was attempting to crawl away unobserved, but he didn't make it very far. Donovan calmly walked over, and bludgeoned the man to death with the butt of the shotgun. He had been worried about his actions today having repercussions with the Lord, but by the end he convinced himself it was all in service of his congregation, so he could do what needed to be done. Ultimately, he would be forgiven. The DA and Donovan did a quick search of both cars. Each started with the trunk. Donovan couldn't open the one on the first car, since it had been welded shut by the heat of the incendiary device.

"Over here!" the DA yelled.

He had checked the footwell of the backseat of the second car and found their prize. Donovan ran over, and the two men took turns lifting the gold into the car the DA had been driving. Both men were sweating and panting when it was done, but they had been successful. Together they hopped in the car, and the DA drove onto the sidewalk to avoid the Caltrops. He deftly negotiated all obstacles, and soon they were on the street headed toward salvation.

Three police cars had been waylaid near the corner. Officers stood about with confused looks on their faces. One of them held a caltrop in his hand and continued to study it. The DA accelerated past them without stopping. It didn't matter if they got a read of the plate. He and Donovan were going to ditch the car before they split up the gold. As the car gained in speed, the Police opened fire. The car took more damage, but it continued to move forward and took Donovan and the DA out of harm's way.

***

The massacre made the papers and lingered on everyone's mind for a few days afterward. However, it was quickly replaced by another. The Division of Investigation spent days and weeks tracking the perpetrators, but they were unable to close the case. Hoover had gotten an earful from the administration, but he knew there would be opportunities to make up for it. There was always going to be a need for his and the Division's services. The men who'd pulled off what had been referred to as The Kansas City Heist were never apprehended, but a file continued to remain open on the case.

United States : December 5th, 1933

FTER RECONCILING THE FAILURE OF Prohibition, Congress ratifies the Twenty-First Amendment of the Constitution which repealed the prohibition of the transport and sale of alcohol. The end of prohibition drastically reduced the impact of organized crime and corruption. In 1934 Alcoholics Anonymous was founded to help people with drinking problems.

United States : 1934 - 1935

DURING THIS TIME PERIOD, THE FOLLOWING *outlaws were killed by law enforcement agents. The tracking of these criminals and the meting out of justice, during The Great Depression, also helped to establish the Federal Bureau of Investigation.*

John Dillinger *was killed July 22nd, 1934. He had led a gang of robbers who known as 'The Terror Gang', and 'The Dillinger Gang', who robbed a grand total of twenty-four banks and four police stations during The Great Depression. Dillinger had also escaped from jail twice; once, with the assistance of 'Baby Face 'Nelson. At one point, he was considered to be Public Enemy Number 1 in the United States.*

'Pretty Boy' Floyd *was killed July 23rd, 1934. He, and his gang, had robbed a series of banks. During his reign, he was also labeled Public Enemy Number 1 in the United States.*

Bonnie and Clyde *were killed May 23rd, 1934. During The Great Depression, Bonnie and Clyde had been romantically linked outlaws who, along with their gang, robbed banks, gas stations, and stores.*

'Baby Face' Nelson *was killed Nov 27th, 1934. Nelson had been responsible for killing more Bureau agents than any other outlaw during the Depression. He had been a prolific bank robber and aided John Dillinger during one of his escapes from jail. Nelson had also been given the moniker of Public Enemy Number 1 in the United States.*

'Ma' Barker *was killed Jan 16th, 1935. She had been the mother of multiple outlaws who had committed a series of robberies during The Great Depression as the Barker-Karpis Gang. She had been the criminal matriarch and masterminded her sons 'criminal endeavors.*

During this era, two other criminals were captured and sentenced to serve time in prison.

'Machine Gun' Kelly *had been a bootlegger but was most well-known for the kidnapping of businessman Charles F. Urschel. Kelly surrendered to the FBI on September 26th, 1933 and was sentenced to life in prison. He served 17 years in Alcatraz and was moved to Leavenworth prison after that. He died from a heart attack on July 18th, 1954.*

Alvin Karpis *had been a leader of the Karpis-Barker gang, and was the final outlaw to be thought of as Public Enemy Number 1 in the United States. More importantly, he was also the only Public Enemy to be captured alive. He was captured in New Orleans in 1936 and served a lengthy prison sentence in Alcatraz from 1936-1962. Karpis was paroled in 1969 and died in Spain from what was ruled to be a suicide in 1978. The capture of Alvin Karpis signaled the end of the reign of the depression era gangster. Other outlaws and gangsters who were killed or captured before or during The Great Depression were 'Legs' Diamond, 'Maddox' Call, 'Jelly' Nash, and 'Dutch' Schultz. Al Capone was sentenced and transferred to Alcatraz penitentiary. His mental faculties were eroded by the effects of syphilis. He was released from prison in 1939. He would die from a stroke and a cardiac arrest over successive days in 1947.*

The Purple Gang from Detroit fell apart due to convictions of three of their leaders in 1931. The Kansas City Organization and the Chicago Outfit continue to operate in one capacity or another. The Weintraub syndicate went legitimate after World War 2.

June 23rd, 1937

"THREE, FOUR, THREE," HAM SAID.

He watched his new protégé rip a combination on the heavy bag. The refurbished bag took the blows and swayed, but the chain did not creak. Ham looked around the recently renovated gym and thought of Ezra for the first time in a while. Ham had been in his office, seated at his desk, when he'd received the letter. He had already read about Ezra's exploits, but the letter filled out all of the details which hadn't been in the paper. Also included was a cashier's check made out to Ham from a bank overseas.

It had been a long time since Ham had been in the ring, and an even longer time since he'd been knocked unconscious, but reading the amount on the check was akin to absorbing a devastating overhand right. He had to read the number a few times before it finally sank in and made sense. Not only would he be able to save the gym, but he could renovate the place. He also wouldn't have to worry about money for a long time. The letter stated that Ezra had left instructions, if he didn't survive the heist, for his share of the money to go to Ham.

Over the next few months, after he got the letter and the check, Ham made preparations to renovate the gym. It was easy enough to find labor, and after a month or so of work the place looked almost brand new. As times got better, more people returned until the gym was back to full capacity. It got to the point where Ham realized he might have to start turning people away.

"Three more times," Ham said.

The protégé went back to the bag. He was a young

and stringy kid, but he possessed deceptive power.

A few days after the massacre, Ezra's body had been interred at Elmwood Cemetery. Ham had watched the burial from a distance. No friends or family attended. Instead, the small group of onlookers was made up solely of municipal workers and G-men. Ham felt conflicted; he was ecstatic about the money, but he also missed the company of his friend.

Ham was lost in his memory when he was interrupted by the boxer.

"What now?" the protégé asked.

"Take a breather," Ham said.

***

"Is it possible to do the wrong things for the right reasons?" Donovan asked.

He waited for the parishioners to digest what he had said. It had been almost four years since the massacre in Kansas City. He'd had to leave the country for a little while, and during his absence he'd lost the church. But it was a small price to pay in the service of the lord. He found solace in thinking about the opportunities which awaited him once he returned. While he was out of the country, he trekked through Europe, spent time at various cathedrals, and decided to walk The Way of St. James. He began his journey in Leon and ended in Santiago de Compostela.

Along the way, he befriended pilgrims from all walks of life. He preached the gospel at all turns. When enough time had elapsed, and it was safe, he returned to America and settled in the Pacific North West. He erected a new church and had enough money squared away to see it tended to throughout his lifetime. It didn't take very long for him to attract a sizable congregation. Donovan lit his pipe and picked up his sermon again.

"Most people will tell you it is impossible. However, what are 'the wrong reasons?' And, if you are doing things in service of the lord to spread his word…"

He let his words trail off and looked out at the sea of people all nodding in agreement. It was a humid day as well, so many of the parishioners were cooling themselves with fans.

"Let us think about the following passages and reflect."

Donovan recalled the following verses from memory.

"In Psalms 96:3 the bible reads 'Declare His glory among the nations, His wonders among all peoples.' Matthew 24:14 'And this gospel of the kingdom will be preached in all the world as a witness to all the nations, and then the end will come.' Mark 16:15 'And He said to them, 'go into all the world and preach the gospel to every creature.'"

Donovan paused yet again for emphasis, and to let people catch up to him.

"Do these commands not carry great weight?" he added.

It had been a rhetorical question, so no one in the audience spoke, but again many of them nodded their head in agreement. Donovan stopped. He extinguished his pipe and replaced it in his pocket. A newly painted portrait of Christ had been displayed above the doorway and observed Donovan as he continued with his sermon.

***

"What shall we do today?" the DA said. He put down his coffee and eagerly anticipated his wife's response. They were seated in chairs on the balcony of the second floor of their home in Rio De Janeiro, which overlooked the water of the Atlantic Ocean. Below them, they could hear the gentle sound of the waves lapping the shore.

At the scene of the massacre, the DA and Donovan had split the gold; the DA took three bars, and Donovan took two. They left the remaining bars at the agreed dead drop. Owens and Anderson could retrieve their shares in their own time. The DA accepted that both Liu and Ezra had been killed, but he would not allow himself to mourn them; at least not yet. He needed to stay focused. Once they had their shares, they ditched the car a few miles away and bid each other good luck. Both of them knew they would never see the other again. The DA watched Donovan walk away until he was a dot on the horizon. Then, he himself went directly to the station to board a train to New York and meet up with his wife.

Before the heist, he had spoken to each of the men individually to discuss their 'last will and testament', should things go foul. Ezra had wanted to leave 'Zeke' some money, but the DA would not accept his brother's gesture. He had argued it would be pointless since he would have his own share. So, Ezra decided he would leave all his money to Ham. The DA already had Ham's address. Once he'd deposited the gold, he would get a cashier's check drawn out for the amount and send it along with a letter which would explain everything.

The train ride took a day and a half. The DA must have checked on the gold at least fifty times to make certain it hadn't miraculously vanished. He took his meals in his train compartment, but otherwise he slept most of the time. While initially he imagined it would be difficult, he ended up falling asleep almost instantly any time he had rested his head. His wife met him at the train station, and for a long time they embraced. The DA's sister-in-law stood nearby, but she waited until husband and wife had finished their greeting before she offered her salutations. The three of them drove to the sister's apartment. Laura had already packed her belongings which had been stowed with a porter. The DA got the sense during the car ride that his wife's visit had been an uneasy time, and when he wasn't invited upstairs it only served to confirm his suspicion. His sister-in-law had agreed to drive them to the pier where they could catch their ship, and though it wasn't due to disembark for a few hours, everyone seemed relieved to head there right away. They said their goodbyes to each other, and though they all agreed it would be wonderful to reunite very soon, the DA knew deep down it would never happen. In fact, the odds were pretty good that this would be the last time the three of them would ever see each other.

Laura squeezed his hand, and he was back on the balcony.

"Why don't we finish our coffee and go for a walk on the beach?" Laura said. She had continued to improve more every day and was almost back to being her old self. Though it didn't seem possible, she looked like she had grown younger and more beautiful since they had reached Brazil. Ultimately, she had managed to avoid any lasting effects from her ordeal, or so it seemed to the DA.

"Sounds terrific," he said.

He sipped at his drink and picked up the paper. It had been touch and go for a while as the pressure had mounted to clean up organized crime, but once they repealed prohibition the Division of Investigation's focus had changed, and the DA ceased to worry. He knew he and Laura would be safe in Rio, and it would be a long time before they returned to the United States, if they went back at all. Once they had settled, the DA allowed himself the opportunity to mourn his brother and Liu. Eventually, he was able to process everything, and he swore to himself one day he would have Liu's body exhumed and sent back to his family in China where he could have a proper burial.

The DA finished his coffee and laid the paper on the table. He leaned back in his chair and let the sun work on him for a moment. When he looked over at his wife, he noticed she had finished her coffee.

"Shall we?" he said and stood up.

"We shall." He took her hand and helped her out of her seat, and together they headed to the beach to walk along the surf.

****

"Como se dice?" asked Owens' wife. She tried her best to say it the way he did, but her accent had made it difficult. "Lancashire Hotpot," Owens said.

They were in the kitchen of their house. He was standing directly behind her, holding her close with his hands wrapped round her waist. She held a cookbook in her hands and was busy looking through the pages for the recipe.

"No lo Veo."

"Es bueno," Owens replied.

His wife put the cookbook on the counter and turned to face her husband. She kissed him and they remained interlocked for a moment. Owens broke away and rested his hand on his wife's stomach.

"Como esta?" Owens asked.

"Esta tranquillo esta noche," his wife replied.

Owens knelt down and kissed his wife's stomach. She was due in another four months, and while they didn't know the sex, he assumed he was going to have a son. Regardless, it didn't matter.

Owens had never given up on the idea of moving to an island if he made it out alive, so he made his way to the coast and boarded a ship to Puerto Rico. He'd laid low for a while and got a job working at a distillery which produced rum. He became fluent in Spanish within the year, and married one of the local women who lived in a village nearby. Though he didn't have to work, he enjoyed the job and decided he would keep the gold to be used only in case of emergencies. Along with Anderson's share, the gold was hidden beneath floorboards in Owens' living room. He had thought about Anderson often. Owens wished he'd have been able to do more for his friend. He had been successful in removing the bullet, and most likely saving his life, but he had to leave Anderson on the rooftop as the police had managed to get by the caltrops and had begun to ascend on the scene.

He believed his actions in leaving his friend unconscious on the rooftop to be a form of betrayal, and he never forgave himself. At night, long after his wife was asleep, Owens would go into the backyard and stare at the moon. If he had believed in God, he might have offered a prayer and asked for forgiveness. Tonight was no different. He went into the yard and sat on a chair and stared up at the moon. It was silent for a while except for the sound of the cicadas and the wind. The humidity was particularly thick this evening. Owens dragged a kerchief over his brow.

He went back inside the house and poured himself a glass of rum. He would have preferred rye, but he had cases of the stuff from work. He took a knife from the drawer, cut the seal, and poured himself three fingers worth. He sat back down in the chair outside. It had been a long time since he had outwardly acknowledged his friend, but for some reason, alone in the yard, he felt compelled to do so. He held up his drink so it blocked out the moon. First, he said a few words commemorating his luck. Then, he offered thanks for his wife and child. Finally, he sent condolences to Liu and Ezra and hoped the rest of his cohorts were enjoying the fruits of their labor. Before he could say anything about Anderson, his voice grew somber. This was a side of himself which rarely made an appearance, even if no one else was around. Suddenly, the words poured forth; it had been a long time since he had spoken openly like this. The eulogy lasted for a full minute. When he finished speaking, he took a long pull. The Rum burned but turned sweet as it always did. Owens looked at the moon. Perhaps Donovan would have tried to convince him there was a sign in the heavens. Then a voice broke the silence.

"That was beautiful," the voice said from the darkness.

Owens immediately had his Colt in his hand and pointed it in the voice's direction

"Careful with that thing," the man said and emerged from the shadows by the far wall which enclosed the property.

"You're liable to kill me, and I'll never be able to collect my money," Anderson said.